NO CURTAIN CALL

Also by Alice Zogg

Stand-Alone Mysteries
The Ill-Fated Scientist
Accidental Eyewitness
A Bet Turned Deadly

R. A. Huber Mysteries

Evil at Shore Haven
Guilty or Not
Murder at the Cubbyhole
Revamp Camp
Final Stop Albuquerque
The Fall of Optimum House
The Lonesome Autocrat
Tracking Backward
Turn the Joker Around
Reaching Checkmate

NO CURTAIN CALL

ALICE ZOGG

This book is a work of fiction.

Published by Aventine Press
55 East Emerson St.
Chula Vista CA 91911
www.aventinepress.com

ISBN: 978-1-59330-959-6

Library of Congress Control Number: 2019907817
Library of Congress Cataloging-in-Publication Data
No Curtain Call / Alice Zogg
Printed in the United States of America

To my granddaughter, Sarah, who loves theater

CREDITS

Credit is due to Patricia Smiley for giving me tips on police procedures. I am lucky to have a high school teacher as my son-in-law who answered questions about campus life. Thank you, Sam. Granddaughter Sarah shared her insider experience with high school theater in general and her love for musicals in particular. Mark, my other son-in-law, gave tips relating to playing a round of golf. Again, Gayle Bartos-Pool did an excellent job of editing. I appreciate your good eye for detail, Gayle. I could never do without my daughter Franziska's proofreading skills. Last but not least, I thank my husband, Wilfried, for being a good sport by keeping me company when scouting out the location for the fictional private high school I had in mind.

PROLOGUE

Opening night of the musical *Woeful,* performed by the high school drama class, drew to its melodramatic conclusion. The character Peterus stood at center stage, belting out the final victory solo, his head held high in triumph.

With the last note vibrant and soaring, his rival, Aurelius, stepped out from the shadows of the stage scenery, proclaiming, "You won, but I will not permit it. We shall perish together!"

And with a swift movement, he pulled out a dagger from within his robe and stabbed Peterus in the heart. As the latter staggered and collapsed, clutching his chest, the character's archenemy turned the weapon on himself and with a shrieking outcry also fell to the ground. The two actors lay side by side when the curtain came down.

Moments later - - amid thunderous applause from the audience - - a stage crew member rushed over to Peterus, shouting, "Hey Jim, get up for curtain call!"

The curtain was not raised and there were no final bows from the performers. Instead, the drama teacher and director appeared, announcing, "We have a medical emergency. Is there a doctor in the audience?"

Three-and-a-half years later

CHAPTER 1

The call from Tho Hoàng on Monday morning, November 5, came as a complete surprise. We had not seen or heard from each other in over three-and-a-half years. In the meantime, our lives had changed drastically. Tho had lost his only son, and a couple months before that, I had lost a kidney and part of my left leg in the line of duty as a homicide detective of the L. A. County Sheriff's Department. Tho and I used to play racquetball twice a week, a sport I had to give up after becoming disabled.

After the initial hellos, Tho said, "Sorry for not keeping in touch. When you first got injured, I didn't want you to feel bad about not being able to play racquetball, and the longer I waited, the less I got up the nerve to call."

"Don't sweat it," I said. "Are you still playing?"

"Sure, I found a couple of opponents. Some days we play cut-throat and others one-on-one games."

I paused, not knowing how best to continue. Other than sending a sympathy card after learning of his son's tragic death, I had kept quiet too.

"Tho," I said, "I'm to blame for not keeping in touch. I was at a loss of what to say after what happened at the Citadel High School."

"That's why I'm calling. My wife and I are sure our Jim did not overdose or commit suicide. The authorities have long closed the case, calling it an accidental death. But we cannot let it rest. Please, Nick, look into it for us."

I protested, "I no longer work for the Sheriff's Department, nor did I at the time of your son's passing."

"I know, but you must still have connections. I want to hire you as a private detective."

To which I replied, "I'm not a private investigator. Whatever gave you that idea?"

There was urgency as he pleaded, "Of course you're not, but you know how to conduct a homicide investigation. Please do this for us. My wife is a shadow of her former self. She cannot shake her grief. We need to get closure."

"Are you telling me you suspect your son was murdered?"

"Yes, I am."

Stunned, I agreed to meet with him to get details but did not make any promises as to whether or not I would take him up on his request.

After hanging up, I thought about Tho for a long time. When in their early twenties, he and his wife sailed from Vietnam to the USA in 1990 with the last wave of new immigrants. Now, 28 years later, his accented English was good, and he'd worked hard to assimilate to his new homeland. He owned a small convenience store near downtown Burbank. I did not know much else about him since our friendship had revolved around the racquetball court. The Hoàngs' son, Jim, was born in the United States. He had died of an opioid overdose on stage - - of all places - - during a musical performance at the prestigious private Citadel High School.

I shook my head. He wants to hire me as a private detective. Is that a possibility for me? The idea suddenly made me grin: *Private Eye Nick Fox*. After I was wounded in the line of duty, I had the option of a desk job, working for the Community Relations Office, or settling for early retirement with a pension. I chose the latter and had been trying my hand at all sorts of activities and hobbies in the last three years, but nothing had stuck. My latest venture, writing a book of true crime short stories, was fizzling out already. I'm not meant to sit. Not in an office job nor at my PC, writing down my experience with crime. To be honest with myself, I craved action. Maybe Tho was getting me into a new beginning. And even if it would only be a one-time deal, the least I could do was look into the mysterious death of my friend's son.

CHAPTER 2

Before my meeting with Tho, I wanted to get the official facts, so I called my former partner, Rick, with whom I'd hung out occasionally in the last three-and-a-half years. As expected, he was busy with a case - - in the past, the two of us were always busy with cases - - but he made time for me. Despite the fact that "Rick and Nick" sounded like a team, my ex-partner had always called me by my last name, and still did.

We met at our favorite sports bar that same evening in November. There was a hockey game in progress on one of the big-screen TV's and football on another, but neither of us paid attention.

He asked, "Are you still writing your memoirs?"

"True crime short stories, not memoirs," I corrected. "I've put it on the back burner for now."

He grinned and said, "Now Fox, what the hell is so important that you needed to see me right away?"

I told him about the Hoàngs' plight and that I was willing to do a bit of private investigating, which seemed to amuse him. Then I asked him to dig up the police incident report and coroner's records plus anything else he could find relating to the closed case.

"You don't need me," he said. "You can get the info through the California Public Records Act."

"I don't feel like submitting a request form and then waiting weeks before getting a marginal report. I count on you to give me the whole enchilada, with people's interviews and all."

He eyed me for a couple of seconds, then stated, "Researching stuff dating back over three years is a tall order, but I see you're serious about getting involved and there's no talking you out of it."

"Affirmative. Do we have a deal?"

"I'll see what I can do," he said, and I gave him the date, the victim's name, and cause of the alleged accident.

He got up, saying, "I've got to run," and was gone. I finished my beer, paid for our drinks and left also.

Rick and I had complemented each other as detective partners. His laid-back attitude had had a calming effect on my compulsive nature. But most importantly, we always had had each other's back. On the day of my misfortune, our department was short-handed. Rick was vacationing, and instead of waiting for another officer to get assigned to me, I thought I could handle a case on my own. That was a wrong assumption. I was careless, letting a suspect sabotage my car. In the split second before I lost consciousness after the explosion, a thought popped into my head: Thank God Rick isn't here and can't get hurt.

The only time the two of us talked about my injuries and consequent disability was on the occasion of his visit to the hospital following my surgery and amputation. Since then, what I like most about my ex-partner is that he treats me exactly the way he always did. No trace of pitying or babying. Unlike some other people, he knows that I am the same Nick Fox minus a leg and kidney.

Three days later, Rick e-mailed me, stating, "Attached is the information you requested. As is evident from the reports, Jim Hoàng died of an opioid overdose. I studied all data, and in my opinion it was an accidental overdose. There are no red flags that point to suicide or homicide."

Attached were copies of the police incident report submitted by Sergeant Anna Diego, the coroner's autopsy findings, and a list of interviewed witnesses with their statements. I downloaded all that data onto my tablet, which I planned to carry with me during the investigation.

CHAPTER 3

Everyone has a past. Mine is rather simple. I grew up in a small town in the San Fernando Valley of Southern California. I studied criminology at a junior college, passed the requirements and worked as sheriff's deputy for three years, then was promoted; first to sergeant, and later to lieutenant, doing criminal investigative work.

I turned 47 last month, am six foot tall, with blue eyes and light brown hair mixed with grey. I was married but it didn't last. We had several issues. It turned out that my gorgeous, younger ex-wife was needy and demanding to the extreme, hating my long work hours. She commanded constant attention, which I was unable and unwilling to give. Her idea of how to bring up our son differed from mine. Consequently, she undermined my authority every chance she got. I suspected that she had affairs - - which I'm sure she felt was the result of my neglect - - but I could not prove it.

A divorce was inevitable. So ten years ago, we called it quits. We divided the profit from the sale of our house and other belongings and went our separate ways. My former spouse, and at the time seven-year-old son, relocated to the East Coast where her roots are, and I moved into a condominium in Burbank. My ex remarried and gave birth to twins. As far as I know, she lives with my son and her new family happily ever after.

My son is a junior in high school now. We talk on the phone or skype, but his visits to California and my trips east are rare. My parents moved to a retirement community in Arizona where they seem to enjoy spending their golden years. My sister, and only sibling, lives in Colorado with a husband and two kids. This all means that I'm unattached, in the true sense of the word.

I've taken up playing golf lately, a sport that suits my current physical ability. Besides racquetball, I also used to ski and mountain bike. Nowadays, I play a round of golf on a regular basis. Before my mishap, I had had a few girlfriends, but at present I've distanced myself from the dating scene. I don't want to be pitied.

From a practical point of view, I've adjusted well to my shortcomings. I can easily live with just one kidney and have become comfortable with my artificial limb. The above-knee prosthetic leg attaches to the stump and fits well. Physical therapy had been essential as a new amputee and artificial limb wearer, and even now I do daily stretches, making sure I can straighten my hip and leg. The prosthesis comes off to sleep and shower; other than that, I treat it as if it were my own flesh. Walking down stairs is still tricky, but I'm getting better at it and eventually the task will become routine. Since only the left leg is affected, I have no problem driving a car with automatic transmission.

CHAPTER 4

Tho stood behind the counter wringing up a customer's items at the cash register when I entered his convenience store. He saw me and called to his wife, who was in the process of stocking the shelves. I figured that Tho must be close to 50. From a distance he had the same youthful appearance as during our racquetball days. A full head of black hair, inquisitive dark, slanted eyes, and a compact lean body. Up close, I noticed grief lines around his eyes and mouth.

As soon as the customer left, he shook my hand and then introduced me to Lan Hoàng. This was the first time I'd met Tho's wife, so could not make a "before and after" comparison. What I perceived, though, was a petite, pretty Asian woman with what seemed like a permanent sad expression. Tho told her to mind the store for a while and then led me through a back door to his office, which amounted to no more than a cubbyhole in the corner of the storage room, furnished with a small desk and two straight-back chairs.

I opened my tablet, showing him copies of the police and coroner's reports and the statements from several witnesses, mainly high school kids who had been part of the cast in the musical.

I stated, "It all looks straightforward as far as I can tell. I know Sergeant Anna Diego, the main investigating detective of your son's case, personally. She's competent and methodical."

"She was nice and treated us with respect," Tho remarked, "but she may have missed something."

"Tho, I'm willing to look into this, but my conclusion may amount to nothing different than the status quo."

"I'm aware of that. All I ask is that you try. I'm 100 percent sure that my son neither took drugs - - opioids or any other - - nor committed suicide."

"Fair enough," I said. "Tell me first what kind of student Jim was and with whom he used to hang out in the days and weeks before opening night of the musical."

My friend took a deep breath and said, "He was an 'A' student with a grade point average of 4.4. He took all advanced placement classes, was president of the math and computer science club, participated on debate teams, and had enrolled in many other extracurricular activities. We were immensely grateful that Citadel High School granted us financial aid for Jim's tuition; otherwise we could have never afforded to give him this great opportunity. The very day of his death, he received the news of being accepted to UC Irvine on a full scholarship."

Tho sighed and continued, "To be honest, I did not like the idea of him taking the drama class. I thought it was a waste of time, especially since he excelled in math and science. His girlfriend talked him into drama and theater stuff and suggested he try out for the lead part in the musical."

I checked the list of names on my tablet and interrupted, "Would that be Melissa Van der Molen?"

"Yes, her," he nodded. "Anyhow, I let him join the drama class as long as he could keep up his grades. Anything less than an 'A' was not acceptable."

He continued, "As for the kids he hung out with during his senior year, it was mainly the girlfriend and other drama students. In the two months before *Woeful*, most of his free time was taken up with rehearsals."

Again, I glanced at the list of witnesses in one of the reports and read their names aloud: Burt Trolley, Alex Topalian, Melissa Van der Molen, Mike Higginson, Andrew Baldoni, and Nelson Montagu.

I asked, "Were all these students of Citadel High School and had they been part of the cast in the musical?"

Tho replied, "I think so but can't be sure. Except for Melissa, I hadn't met any of the others. I saw them on stage at the premiere but couldn't tell who the characters were in real life. Oh, and the last person you mentioned, Nelson Montagu, was not a student. He was, and as far as I know still is, the drama teacher."

"Did Jim have other friends, besides the ones in drama class?"

"His best friend, ever since starting at Citadel as a freshman, was Sean Brooks. The two boys were inseparable."

"What about girlfriends before Melissa?" I wanted to know.

"I don't think he had any." As an afterthought, he added, "There was always Zoe, of course."

"Who's Zoe?"

"She's the daughter of our next-door neighbors. Zoe was never his girlfriend but more like a best buddy, ever since Kindergarten."

I paused. There was no way around it, I needed to hear the events of the tragedy in his words.

I said, "What comes next is painful for you, but I must know the details. Tell me exactly what happened on stage during Jim's performance."

Tho nodded and said, "As I told you, I was not enthusiastic about Jim's drama activities. Naturally, we went to see the musical he was starring in, so I closed shop early on that Saturday, but had no great expectations."

I interrupted again, "By 'we,' you mean you and your wife?"

"Yes, and our daughter Jennifer and my mother came too."

He resumed, "Other than occasionally hearing him in the shower, I had no idea Jim could sing. We certainly never paid for singing lessons. I learned later from my mother, who lives with us, that his talent was self-taught. Before auditioning for the part of Peterus, he listened to the professional *Woeful* musical on YouTube over and over again, and practiced singing the character Peterus's solos."

Tho tried hard not to get teary-eyed but didn't succeed as he continued, "We were blown away by Jim's performance. Not only did he have a great voice, but our introverted son had a presence and self-assurance on stage. His solo in the last act was amazing."

He blinked and said, "I don't know if you are familiar with *Woeful,* but at the end, the character Aurelius stabs first Peterus, then himself. As the curtain came down, both lay on the stage floor, pretending to be dead. We were waiting for the curtain to go up again for curtain call, but that never happened. Instead, the lights went on and Mr. Montagu appeared, asking for a doctor. Minutes later, he announced that everyone in the audience should leave, except for the Hoàng family. Then we were rushed behind the curtain on stage, where we found the paramedics working on our son."

Realizing that Tho had trouble controlling his emotion, I said, "Take your time."

He stared at the wall behind me, no doubt re-living the scene as he said, "It was horrible to watch Jim's limp body, labored breathing, and blue lips and fingernails. The medics mentioned a slow heartbeat and low blood pressure. They kept working on him while putting him on a stretcher and then he was carted off in an ambulance. I followed it to the hospital in my own car, and Lan drove there in Jim's Toyota."

There was pain in his eyes when he added, "We learned later that he had stopped breathing altogether in the ambulance on the way to the hospital. They could not revive him."

We stayed silent for a long while. Then I said, "Are you aware that the coroner added a separate note to his report?"

Tho shook his head.

I reached for my tablet, found what I was looking for, and read aloud:

"*The victim would most likely have been able to be saved if administered Naloxone in time, the antidote to an opioid overdose. There is no indication that the deceased was a habitual user.*"

Tho said, "One of the paramedics asked if my son used drugs and I told him, *absolutely not.*"

"The coroner's findings state that Jim died from an overdose of hydrocodone, better known as Vicodin, which is an opioid painkiller."

"I know," Tho admitted, "but I'm positive that he did not swallow those pills willingly. Someone must have drugged him, slipping it into his beverage, or something."

"Did you have painkillers prescribed for adults in your house?"

"No, we don't believe in taking strong medication; we use natural remedies for illness or pain."

"In the report is also mentioned that there was alcohol in his system."

Tho stated with conviction, "My son did not drink alcohol."

I finally asked, "Who would have had a motive for killing your son?"

"I have no idea. He was a good kid."

I said, "That's all I needed from you for now. I'll interview everyone involved, starting with your wife. Go back to minding your store and tell her to come see me, please."

He protested, "I've told you all we know. Lan can't add anything more, I'm sure."

"I'd like to talk with her, regardless."

Tho wanted to discuss my fee. I told him that I would not accept any money, excluding possible expenses. I had two reasons for doing the investigation free of charge. First and foremost, I wanted to help my friend out. Second, I was not licensed and didn't want to deal with reporting any extra income to the IRS.

CHAPTER 5

Reflecting on what questions to ask Lan Hoàng - - wanting to spare her the pain of re-experiencing what I had already covered with Tho - - I was unaware that she had silently entered the room and shut the door behind me.

I almost jumped when she said, "Yes?"

"Mrs. Hoàng, Tho has given me an in-depth account of what happened to your son. I won't go over the tragic event again, but I'd like to get some insight from you as the boy's mom."

She bowed her head in agreement, then said, "Call me Lan."

"Okay, Lan. So tell me about Jim. What kind of a kid was he?"

She lit up and stated, "Our Jim gave us nothing but joy, from the time he was born until the end. He was intelligent and things came easy to him. Still, he studied hard to keep up good grades. Even though he was busy with after school activities and homework, he made time to earn his spending money by tutoring and walking people's dogs. Since Tho and I tended to the store, Jim was in charge of his younger sister until we got home. Not an easy task, since our Jennifer is a bit of a rebel."

I said, "I understand that Melissa Van der Molen was his girlfriend. What can you tell me about her?"

"Melissa was a sweet girl but, like most students at Citadel, came from money."

"And that's not good?"

"Nothing wrong with it, but she gave Jim ideas we couldn't afford. Like going to professional theater performances and musicals. And for instance, her parents bought her a brand-new BMW. Our Jim drove to school in his ancient Toyota Corolla."

I asked, "I assume they met because they had classes together?"

"No," she replied, "Jim was listed as tutor on the school's bulletin board. At the end of their junior year, Melissa hired him to tutor her in math. They quickly became boyfriend and girlfriend. As I said, she was sweet and lovely to look at. The girl was heartbroken after what happened."

"Are you keeping in touch with her?" I asked.

"In the beginning, yes, but then she moved on, which is only natural for a young person. She attends UC Irvine." And Lan's sad eyes met mine as she added, "They'd been planning to go there together."

I asked, "Do you happen to have her phone number or address?"

"Not anymore. In her freshman college year she lived in the university's dorm but then moved into an apartment and we lost contact. Her parents live in La Cañada Flintridge. They might be willing to give you her number."

"There can't be too many Van der Molens in that town," I remarked.

She suddenly grabbed my arm in despair and cried out, "You help us clear our son's name and get justice!" And before I could formulate any response, her eyes got moist and she stated, "As Catholics, we're supposed to forgive our enemies. How can I forgive my enemy if I don't even know who he is?"

I gently said, "So you share your husband's belief that your son was murdered?"

"Yes, but I think it was an accident."

"It can't be both."

"What I mean is, the killer accidentally slipped the pills into something that Jim ate or drank, but they were meant for someone else."

"That's a theory which hadn't occurred to me," I remarked.

Lan assured me, "Everyone liked our Jim. Nobody had a reason to murder him."

CHAPTER 6

The Hoàngs lived in a modest four-bedroom, two-bath single-level home in a residential area not far from downtown Burbank. On Saturday, November 10, I had an appointment to talk with their daughter, Jennifer. She led me into the dining area of their living room, where we settled facing each other across the table. A mane of dark hair outlined her angular face, and there was pure spunk reflected in her brown eyes. The young woman radiated a strong vitality, and I sensed that she willed herself to sit still. I had learned from Tho that his daughter attended a local community college and planned a transfer to a major university after two years.

Before I could start the interview, she said, "So what do you want to know about Jim's death that my parents haven't already told you?"

This young person gets straight to the point, I thought. Interesting! Aloud I said, "Before we go into that, tell me what your brother was like."

"He was a frickin' genius. Straight 'A's and an SAT score of 1590. Jim was faultless. And it turned out that he could even sing."

She seemed to realize how her words sounded and added, "Don't get me wrong. I loved my brother and miss him, but he was just too perfect."

"And you couldn't keep up with him?" I asked.

"Oh, I wasn't interested in keeping up nor wouldn't have wanted to try. I doubt it was expected of me. He was the first born and a boy."

"What do you mean by that?"

"After my father, Jim was the next person of authority in our household." And she blurted, "My parents have tried to fit in since day one, giving us American names and all, but can't let go of their traditional Vietnamese shit." She seemed embarrassed over her language and said, "Sorry! That slipped out."

"So while your parents tended to their store, your brother was in charge of you, correct?"

"Yes, and I had to mind him, even though he was only two years older than me."

"And you resented that?"

"Not really," she said.

"But?"

"It's just that he always got the breaks. My parents put all their eggs in one basket. They applied for and received financial aid for him to go to Citadel High School and then he got a scholarship to attend UC Irvine. I went to the local public high school and am now going to a community college."

"A bit of hard feelings on your part was only natural," I remarked.

She shrugged and said, "Maybe, but I loved him."

There was loud music coming from some other room in the house. Jennifer jumped up and closed the door, which made it bearable, but we could still hear the blaring sounds of a commercial tune.

"Sorry, that's my grandma's TV. She's hard of hearing."

I said, "You mentioned that your brother was faultless. Come now, everyone has faults. Tell me about Jim's."

She thought about it and then said, "I don't know if you can call it a fault but he was gullible. It was paradox that such a brain could also be naïve."

"Give me an example."

She grinned and said, "You asked me whether I resented Jim for being in charge. Well, I found ways to work around that. It never occurred to him that I could be lying. He was such a trusting soul and took my word - - and everyone else's, for that matter - - at face value. So if I told him that I was going to such-and-such friend's house but in fact went somewhere I wasn't allowed to go, he never checked up on me."

"I see. He was easy to manipulate." Then I asked, "What can you tell me about your brother's girlfriend Melissa?"

"She was okay. A bit stuck up but that came with the territory. She was gorgeous, popular, the head cheerleader, and landed leads in plays and musicals."

"How did you know all that since you didn't go to Citadel?"

"Jim tutored her in our house so I knew her. And he talked of her all the time. I wondered what she saw in him other than that he was a brain." She blushed and added, "I mean, I'm sure she could've had her pick of all the boys at her school."

I said, "You were in the audience on Jim's fateful night, correct?"

She nodded and then burst out, "It was a nightmare. When the director asked if there was a doctor around, we had no idea that it was Jim who needed medical help. I soon heard sirens but didn't think anything of it. After being escorted behind the curtain on stage, I started to wonder what the hell was going on. Then I saw the paramedics working on some lifeless body. Suddenly realizing it was Jim, I had to hold a hand over my mouth so I wouldn't puke." She shivered and whispered, "It was a horrific sight."

I gave her a moment to collect herself and then asked, "Now with the passing of time, is it getting a little easier for your family to deal with your brother's death?"

"Not at all," she replied. "This has become a house of mourning. Mom hasn't smiled in over three years and I'm sure Dad blames himself for what happened."

"Why?"

"Isn't it obvious?"

I looked at her and waited.

She stamped her foot in anger and said, "He expected excellence of Jim, who finally caved in under the pressure."

"Are you saying you believe your brother committed suicide?"

"What other possibilities are there? The autopsy showed opioid and alcohol in his system. He never used drugs or drank alcohol. You can't force someone to swallow pills, so murder is out."

"He may have been addicted to opioids without anyone knowing about it," I suggested.

"Tell that to someone easier to fool," she replied.

CHAPTER 7

Jennifer led the way to Mai Hoàng's room, then stood at its open door and yelled, "Hey Grandma! Mr. Fox wants to talk to you."

The TV was still blasting at an earsplitting volume on a Vietnamese channel with a tutorial on *Vovinam,* a form of martial arts. The old lady looked in our direction and pressed the "off" button on her remote. Then there was abrupt silence.

Jennifer said, "You'll have to talk loud, but she understands English. I leave you to it," and was gone.

I raised my voice and said, "Hello, Mrs. Hoàng. Do you know why I'd liked to talk with you?"

She bowed her head and replied, "Tho told me."

She motioned me into a straight-back chair that stood against the wall. She herself sat in a rocker facing the TV. Then she looked me in the eye and announced, "You here to clear family name."

Although she talked in broken English, Mai Hoàng's intention was clear.

"So you don't believe your grandson accidentally overdosed on opioids or killed himself?" I asked, keeping my volume up.

She seemed irate at the suggestion and shouted, "Jim good boy! No drugs, no drink. Suicide a sin. He good boy!"

I touched her arm gently to calm her and said, "I can tell that you and Jim were close."

She nodded and there was a twinkle in her eye as she stated, "He tell me things."

"What kind of things?"

She gave me a blank look and I realized that I forgot to raise my voice. I yelled, "What kind of things did your grandson tell you?"

"Oh, happy or scary."

We're finally getting someplace, I thought, and said, "You mean he was scared of someone?"

She shook her head and corrected, "No, just scary. He tell me, not parents."

"I see. He'd tell you things that he wouldn't tell others, not even his parents."

She nodded.

"So what was he afraid of?"

"Bees, not getting scholarship, and singing in musical."

"Was he allergic to bee stings?"

The old lady gave me another one of her blank looks.

"You said he was afraid of bees."

She explained, "I say he afraid to get 'B' and not 'A'."

"My mistake!" I said. "And by 'singing in musical' you mean that Jim had stage fright?"

"Yes, but on day he die he say 'Okay now, no more scary.'"

"He found a way to get over his stage fright?"

"Yes."

She touched the remote, hinting that she was eager to get back to her TV program.

I said, "Just one more thing, Mrs. Hoàng. I know it is three-and-a-half years later, but do you remember what your grandson's last day was like up until his performance in the evening?"

"I remember. I think about it many days. In the morning he go dress rehearsal. Then he get good news from university and say 'I go tell friends' and drive away. Then he whistling and tell me he no more scary and he get ready and drive to school. My son take us later."

The expression on her face turned to sadness and I quickly said, "You don't need to go on. I know the rest."

"You leave now," she said, and turned the TV back on.

I thanked her for her time but doubted that she heard me over the loud noise coming from the tube.

CHAPTER 8

In the late morning on Monday, November 12, I left my condo in Burbank and drove toward the valley. It was time to have a close look at the crime scene, if indeed there was one. Like most people living in Southern California, I knew of the prestigious Citadel High School but had never set foot on its grounds. Before heading out that morning I did a bit of research and learned several things.

The non-religious, mixed gender private school was known for excellence in teaching academics but had also a reputation of being dedicated to the performing arts. The school's plays and musicals could compete with professional performances in talent and technique. Its campus was relatively small with roughly 400 students, grades 9 through 12, and an average class size of 15. Parents sent their kids to Citadel from all over the southland in hopes of high achievements from their offspring. There was a waiting list to get in. The school had 98% of their students attending college after graduating. It was no surprise that the private institute of learning came with an enormous price tag.

Citadel High School nestled in the northeast part of the San Fernando Valley at the foothills of the Angeles National Forest in an area called Lake View Terrace. There were several options to get there from my residence. I chose driving along Sunland

Boulevard and then taking the I-210 West toward San Fernando, exiting on Wheatland Avenue. The ten-mile drive took only fifteen minutes.

Once on surface streets, I navigated through a residential area - - which to my amazement was horse country - - and then drove onto the short, private road that led up to the school, perched at the foot of the forest. I parked in one of the visitor's spaces in the parking structure, then walked over to the main building.

I paused for a moment at the circular courtyard to take in the view. Immediately above me stretched the mountain range, and below, I had a great view into the valley and the Hansen Dam recreation area. I wondered if the students appreciated the impressive panorama.

My appointment with the school principal, Diana Deschamps, was at 11:30, leaving me a few minutes to find the administration wing, where a secretary walked me to Ms. Deschamps' office. The woman running the school got up from behind her desk and with a pleasant smile came to greet me as I entered. She looked to be about 40, slender, and due to her high heels, her eyes were almost level with mine.

She motioned me into a chair in front of her desk and settled back into hers, saying, "So Mr. Fox, you're here to inquire into the tragic death of our former student, Jim Hoàng?"

"Correct," I replied. "I hope that you knew the boy personally and can tell me about him."

"I'm in charge of a small school and make it my business to get to know all our students personally."

"Excellent!"

Her cell phone rang. She glanced at it and said, "Excuse me for a second, this won't take long," and accepted the call.

The interruption gave me an opportunity to study her more closely. The auburn hair was cut into a chin-length, becoming style, framing her face. Her eyes were green and the full lips, which moments earlier held a warm smile, now bent down at the corners and her entire expression turned into a frown as she listened to the caller.

I couldn't help but overhearing the one-sided dialogue:

"That's no longer my problem! May I remind you that our divorce was final eight months ago?"

She listened for what seemed a long time, then shouted, "Bullshit! Talk to my lawyer," and turned her phone off.

To me she said, "Sorry you had to hear this. Now where were we?"

"No problem. You were about to tell me what kind of a kid Jim Hoàng was."

"Right. Jim was a model student, excelling in all academic subjects. There wasn't a task he couldn't fulfill if he put his mind to it. I learned from our career counselor that he had applied for scholarships to several major universities but had his hopes set on UC Irvine - - a school that, by the way, accepted him on his very ill-fated day."

"Why was that?"

"He qualified," she said with a shrug. I guessed she thought, isn't that obvious?

I said, "I meant what was the reason he chose UC Irvine?"

"Oh, because of its reputation of having an excellent computer science program, a field Jim planned to pursue."

"Makes sense." And I asked, "On a personal note, what did you think of Jim?"

Without hesitation she stated, "Not only did he excel academically, but he was a truly nice kid, following the rules and extending a helping hand to his fellow students. In all his four years with us, he never needed to be disciplined for any reason.

Learning that he overdosed on opioids was a great shock. As a matter of fact, I found it hard to believe."

Her green eyes stared into mine as she added, "You're investigating the matter further?"

"Yes, unofficially. Jim's father wants me to look into it to clear their name."

She nodded and said, "I hope you can, without implying anything worse."

"I think I know what you mean."

"Of course you do! The idea that a student, let alone a faculty member, of our school would resort to murder is unthinkable." And her eyes suddenly clouded with sadness as she said, "I feel for Mr. Hoàng as I've also experienced the loss of a child."

I looked at her in anticipation, but she said no more.

As the silence grew uncomfortable, I inquired, "Did you attend the opening night of the musical and witness Jim's collapse?"

"I did. And it was heartbreaking, even though at first I had no idea what was happening. Like the rest of the audience, I believed that his falling down was part of the act, which it initially was. Only when the boy didn't get up for curtain call, some of the cast members realized that something was wrong and alerted our drama teacher, Nelson Montagu, who had someone call 911 and then informed me. I'm sure you know the rest."

"Can you tell me something that stands out about any of the other students who performed in the musical that year?"

"Nothing comes to mind," she replied and checked her wristwatch, asking, "Is there anything else I can help you with?"

"Not at the moment, but might I trouble you again in the future should things come to light?"

"Absolutely."

"And if you remember anything unusual about Jim or his peers, please give me a call," I said, and gave her my cell phone number.

I got up to leave and said, "Speaking of Mr. Montagu, I'm scheduled to meet with him during lunchbreak. Where is the auditorium?"

She gave me directions and I felt myself dismissed.

An interesting woman, I thought, as I left the administration building and made my way past the classrooms and the gym. As directed, I found the sports field to my right and the auditorium to the left. I caught myself reflecting that I wouldn't mind looking into those green eyes again, given the chance.

CHAPTER 9

Students were dismantling the stage scenery in the auditorium and then carting the disassembled pieces off through a side door. A well-groomed man in his early forties stood at center stage, directing traffic. He was dressed in black flannel trousers and a belted silver blazer, and despite his obvious energy, there seemed not a hair of his out of place.

"Be careful with those lanterns, we might use them again someday," he warned.

"Sure thing, Mr. Drama," one of the students hauling them away replied.

There wasn't another soul in the entire audience section, so I took a seat in center first row and watched the young men and women at work while waiting for Nelson Montagu to arrive.

The immaculate man suddenly looked down at me and hollered, "Are you Nick Fox?"

I nodded.

"Be with you in a moment!"

He took a few more minutes instructing his charge, and when he came to meet me, I asked, "So you're Nelson Montagu? I thought one of the young men called you by a different name."

"Oh, that," he said, "the students call me Mr. Drama. I don't mind. After all, I'm their drama teacher." Not without humor he added, "And since I'm openly gay, I tend to also be a bit dramatic."

Then he said, "Let's go away from the commotion so we can talk," and led me to the last theater row. While we walked up the aisle he noticed my limp but didn't ask me about it, which gave him an A-plus in my estimation.

Once seated, I said, "From what's happening on stage I gather that you recently had a performance."

"That's right. We put on a play in the fall and a musical in the spring. The fall play just ended this weekend with yesterday's matinee as the last show. I have some relaxation time now before auditions start for the casting of the spring musical."

Then he flailed a hand at me and said, "To be honest, I was at first reluctant to give you an interview. When you called I was too busy with the play, but that wasn't the only reason. I spent over three years trying to forget the tragic event and was unwilling to think let alone talk about it, getting the emotions running again. But Ms. Deschamps said we needed to cooperate as we have nothing to hide."

"I appreciate that," I remarked. "Now then, tell me about the musical of three-and-a-half years ago where Jim Hoàng had a lead role."

"Like I mentioned, we put on a play in the fall and a musical in the spring. The musical *Woeful* ran for three consecutive weekends. Premiere night was on a Saturday in April, followed by the Sunday matinee and evening show. The same schedule was held the next weekend, and it ended on the third with just two performances, Saturday night and Sunday matinee."

"I understand that Jim lost his life on opening night. Was *Woeful* not cancelled for the rest of the performances?"

Mr. Montagu paused before he said, "I thought about doing that but then changed my mind. *The show must go on* was the motto that prevailed."

"So you had an understudy for Jim's character?"

"Yes. We had understudies for all three lead characters. They had minor roles in the musical but rehearsed the solo parts of the main characters. This is my usual practice, since I don't want to take chances with one of the leads getting sick."

"As the drama teacher, do you take on the role of director and choreographer when putting on musicals and plays?"

He stated, "Director, yes, but the school hires outside professional choreographers."

"I would imagine that auditions are heard by you as director and also the choreographer, correct?"

"Yes, we are both present, but I make the final decisions."

The drama teacher kept an eye toward the stage while we talked and suddenly shouted, "No, no! That part of the background stays. Don't touch it!"

To me he said, "Sorry."

Getting to the point, I inquired, "What can you tell me about Jim Hoàng?"

"Besides drama, I also teach English. I had Jim in my English class during his sophomore year. He was an exemplary student and possessed leadership ability. I had no idea, though, that he was interested in the performing arts and was surprised when he took drama as a senior. And when he auditioned for the part of Peterus in *Woeful*, I was stunned." The man lifted both arms in the air and proclaimed enthusiastically, "The boy could *sing!*"

"Did you know anything about him personally?" I wanted to know.

"What do you mean?"

"Did he like to party, drink alcohol and occasionally use recreational drugs?"

"No, I couldn't picture him doing any of that and was startled when I learned how he died."

"I understand that there was a stagehand who first noticed that something was wrong with Jim."

"We call them stage crew members, and they're volunteer students. And yes, I remember that particular boy. He was a first-year student then and is now a senior. As a matter of fact, he had a role in this year's musical and also one in the play that just ended."

"Is it possible for me to have a word with him?"

He looked at his watch and stated, "I don't see why not. Lunch break is for another 25 minutes."

He hollered toward the stage, "Someone get a hold of Burt Trolley, please. Try the cafeteria."

As he turned his attention back to me, I said, "Did you know Melissa Van der Molen well?"

"You could say that. She was in my drama class all four years and in all musicals and some of the plays. A pleasant girl and easy to work with."

"Did you know that she and Jim were dating?"

"Yes, there was no secret about that. It was Melissa who got him to take drama in his senior year and urged him to audition for the part in *Woeful*."

I continued, "I have a list of witnesses who were initially interviewed by the authorities - - all students attending Citadel High School at the time - - and believe that they were part of the cast in *Woeful*. I'd like to have this confirmed by you."

I checked the list on my tablet and read their names aloud: "Burt Trolley, Alex Topalian, Melissa Van der Molen, Mike Higginson, and Andrew Baldoni. I know that Melissa had the female lead in the musical, and you just told me about Burt. I'd like you to verify the others."

"You're correct. They were all part of the musical that year. Alex Topalian was Jim's understudy; Mike Higginson sang in a trio together with Melissa and Jim; and Andrew Baldoni was cast as Aurelius, who was Peterus' rival. And I assume you know that Jim was the character Peterus."

"That's all clear, thanks," I said. "And I'm curious, do you know if any of these students are pursuing a theater career now?"

"The only one I know of is Mike Higginson. He's currently enrolled at UCLA in the drama and theater arts program which he plans to major in."

"Are you in contact with him?"

"Yes, we keep in touch." He grinned and added, "I'm always interested in the progress of one of my protégées."

Before I could think of a clever response, a tall, lanky student came rushing up the center aisle toward us. He said, "What's up, Mr. Drama?"

"Mr. Fox here is investigating Jim Hoàng's tragic death and would like your account."

The young man was clearly taken by surprise and gave me a weird look which was hard to read. Was it astonishment, shock, disbelief or fear?

He stared at me for a few seconds, then burst out, "You're starting another investigation after all this time?" And he didn't give me a chance to comment and stated, "After what happened I was interviewed by one of your detectives - - a woman - - and couldn't tell her much."

"I'm not part of the authorities, just looking into the matter privately. I understand that you were the first person who discovered that Jim was in trouble. Please describe what happened."

"Okay. It was at the very end of the musical. Jim was singing his last solo - - I didn't see him since I was backstage - - only heard him. Then I heard Andrew, as Aurelius, saying his last line and knew that the stabbing scene was taking place and they would both be staggering to the floor, pretending to be dead. As soon as the curtain came down, I rushed on stage to remove a prop, before curtain call. I saw Andrew getting up but Jim stayed lying there. I went over to him, trying to make him get up, but he wasn't moving."

He took a deep breath and said, "He looked awful, all slumped and barely breathing. I knew something was terribly wrong and ran to get Mr. Drama."

I said, "Sorry to have made you go through this again. Did you notice anything different in Jim's behavior on his final day before that last scene?"

"No, but then I wouldn't have been aware of it if there had been. I was only part of the stage crew and not anywhere close to him during his entire performance."

I thanked him for his cooperation and he left us.

Unable to think of anything else to ask Nelson Montagu, I ended our interview also. I gave him my number with the request to let me know if something more connected to Jim Hoàng should occur to him.

On the drive home I thought, I learned a lot today but doubt whether any of it helps me in my investigation.

CHAPTER 10

One way or another, I discovered the whereabouts of the former high school students mentioned in the police report. To start, I made a trip to Irvine for a lunch rendezvous with Melissa Van der Molen at UC Irvine's Anthill Pub & Grille at noon on Wednesday of the same week. Although Jim's friend Sean Brooks was not on the police report list and apparently had not been interviewed initially, I learned that the young man was also currently a student at the same university. I had attempted to contact him but he failed to answer my call, which had gone to voicemail.

In case I would be able to locate Sean while at UCI and he would agree to meet me at night, I packed an overnight bag. Traffic to Orange County never being light, I allowed myself plenty of time and left my place at 10:00 a.m. Once in the vicinity of the university, I consulted my googled map of campus locations and stopped to purchase a one-day visitor parking permit at one of the dispensers.

The Anthill Pub was located on the Student Center Terrace, which according to my map was a fair distance's walk from where I'd parked. It was fifteen minutes before the appointed time and I could afford to stride at a comfortable pace to accommodate my left leg. On that mild November day with temperatures in the seventies, I seemed to be the only one out for a leisurely stroll. The students around me all rushed from one place to another on foot or by bicycle.

Melissa stood waiting for me in front of the place. I had described what I looked like and what I was wearing to her over the phone, which proved unnecessary. Although there were lots of people milling around, I was the only middle aged man among them. She had that blonde, blue-eyed, long-legged Nordic look and stepped toward me, saying, "Mr. Fox?"

"You got it. Thanks for making time for me."

We found an empty table by the window, far away from the chatter and glass banging of the bar, and she remarked, "It's never too crowded here for lunch, that's why I suggested it. The place gets hopping in the evenings, though."

We ordered fish tacos, drank bottled water, and began a friendly conversation. I learned that she was a junior, planned to major in biology and then enter a physical therapist program to get her masters degree and license as such. She seemed offended at my comment that physical therapy was a well-paying job and stated that the reason for her seeking it was to help people, not the money. She also mentioned that she had recently moved out of an apartment she'd shared with two other girls and now lived by herself. This got me thinking that money appeared to be no object with her parents and that the young woman I was talking to had no idea what it meant to have to make a living.

I got down to business and said, "Let's get to the reason of why I'm here. Tell me about Jim Hoàng."

"He was my boyfriend in high school, but you know that already." She blinked and said, "I still miss him."

"I've talked to several people, trying to learn what Jim was like, but I'm interested in your account of him. I'm sure you spent a lot of time together, so I'm curious to know your opinion."

She stated, "Everybody probably told you what a brain he was and that's true. He was the smartest person I've ever known, but that's not what impressed me the most. I admired him for his kindness, honesty, and integrity. There wasn't a mean bone in his body. He didn't even see any bad in others. Jim was so trusting that people tended to take advantage, if you know what I mean."

"Yes, I think I do," I remarked.

A bunch of students at the table next to ours were joking and laughing, getting louder and louder. Melissa didn't seem to be bothered by it or the fact that we had to raise our voices to hear one another. I tried to also ignore the unruly group.

I yelled, "I understand that it was you who got Jim interested in performing."

She nodded and confirmed, "One day in the summer before our senior year, I heard him whistling, carrying a perfect tune. So I said, 'I bet you have a great voice. Take drama and audition for the spring musical.' And he did, ending up with a lead role in *Woeful*."

Melissa glanced at me with sad eyes and added, "Jim had a habit of whistling when happy, or if he successfully solved a problem."

There was serenity in her demeanor as she shared, "I was a basket case when I lost Jim. Suddenly my carefree world came to an abrupt end. My parents even hired a shrink to get me over the worst depression. But, *life goes on*, and starting college helped. I've since moved on and have a current boyfriend." She looked me in the eye and continued, "I've left the past behind, and now, since your call, I'm caught back in it again."

"I'm sorry about that," I said, "but there is a chance that Jim's death was no accident and I believe that you want to assist me."

"Absolutely. I owe it to him."

"Good. I need to know the truth. Was Jim dependent on opioids in any shape or form?"

"No way! He didn't even believe in taking any kind of medication when he had a cold. When I learned that he died from an overdose, I didn't believe it for a minute and thought that the coroner must have made a wrong analysis."

I asked, "What about alcohol? Did he occasionally drink any?"

"I'm sure he never did."

"And his friends? Did any of them use drugs or liquor?"

She hesitated and then replied, "I don't think so."

"Melissa, I understand that all you kids were below the legal drinking age three years ago and that illegal drugs were a no-no, but this is not the time to shield anyone. I guarantee that there will be no consequences, but I need to know."

She said, "I think he was just bragging and don't even believe he actually did it, but Jim's best friend told us that he sometimes nipped into his dad's liquor cabinet."

"Would that be Sean Brooks?"

"You are well informed. Yes, it was Sean."

I said, "I understand that he's also a UCI student. Are you two keeping in touch?"

"That's right. He transferred from Pasadena City College this semester. Sean and I supported each other in our grief back in high school. Jim's death was as hard on him as it was on me. In a way it affected him more. Even now, he sometimes has a hard time concentrating and struggles to keep up his grades. We lost contact when I came to Irvine, but now that he's here, we hooked up again."

"So he's your new boyfriend?"

"Oh no, you misunderstand. I have a different boyfriend."

I stated, "I've tried to set up an interview with Sean, but he didn't answer my call."

She checked the time and said, "He has classes later on but is probably eating lunch someplace right now. I'll text him," and she promptly did.

The rowdy students next to us were getting up to leave and we could talk at a normal volume again.

I said, "This is going to be painful, but I do need you to go into details about Jim's last day. Tell me everything you remember about it."

She took a deep breath and started, "On that Saturday morning we had the dress rehearsal, and ..."

I interrupted, "Did you notice anything different about Jim? For example, had he overcome his stage fright?"

She shot me an affronted glance. "What are you suggesting? Jim never had stage fright."

"Sorry! Looks like I've gathered a wrong impression. Please go on."

"After the dress rehearsal we went our separate ways, driving to our homes. In the afternoon he came by my house. You see, we had both learned that very day that we'd been accepted to UCI. Naturally, we hugged and kissed and stuff, so happy that we were going to be together for the next four years."

She blushed, then went on, "He told me that he'd stop by Sean's house on his way home, expecting that he'd also received good news. I learned later that Sean had not been accepted, which was a bummer. He so wanted also to go to UCI. We had to be back at school two-and-a-half hours before the show. Dinner for the cast and crew was provided to us at the auditorium, but I remember eating little, being too excited about performing at opening night."

"A bit of butterflies too?"

"Not really. The dress rehearsal that morning had gone well and I'd had no problem hitting the high notes in my solos, so I was confident. But you want to know about Jim. He only had one slice of pizza, which I'm sure was because he was also too excited to eat much."

"You answered part of my next question as to what kind of food and drink were offered. So you had pizza. And what was there to drink?"

"The choice was water, tea - - hot or iced - - lemonade, and juice, but no milk." She explained, "Milk is not good for the vocal cords, so it should be avoided before singing."

"I take it that you and Jim sat together during the dinner. What kind of beverage did Jim have with his slice of pizza?"

"Water, I think."

"Any dessert?"

"There were cookies, but I don't remember if he went to get one or not. Does it matter?"

"Possibly not," I replied, "but it never hurts to get the details." And I probed further, "Who else was close to him while he ate?"

"There were tons of people around us; I can't remember who exactly. Why would that be important?" Her eyes suddenly opened wide and she exclaimed, "Oh my God! You think someone tampered with his food or drink."

"It's a possibility."

We heard a beep and she pulled her phone out of her purse, checked the text message, and then stated, "Sean is on his way over here." And she continued, "There's not much more I can tell you. Opening night of *Woeful* was a success. Everyone performed well; nobody forgot their lines or sang out of tune, we were all on fire and so was the audience."

Her eyes got moist and her voice shook as she murmured, "I don't want to go into what happened at the end."

"You don't have to, but tell me a bit about what goes on backstage during a play or musical. For instance, what do people do when waiting for their turn to go on stage? How do they know when they're on? Is there a person that holds up a sign with names, announcing *You're next*?"

Despite our grave subject I had made her laugh and she educated me, "They wait quietly in the wings, listening for their cue to go on stage. They have their cue memorized, and it can either be a line in the play, part of the music, a song, some sound effect, or even a motion from something that happens in the play or musical."

"Makes sense." And I inquired, "What are the cast members generally doing during intermission?"

"The cast may get notes from the director or just be hanging out backstage. No one needs to be quiet as there is plenty of noise coming from the audience up front. They also get their costumes and props ready for Act Two."

At that point she waved to someone over my shoulder, and in the next second a young man stood by our table, asking, "What's up, Mel?" Then he noticed me and added, "Oh, you've got company."

She made the introductions. "This is Sean," she said. Then, "Mr. Fox is investigating what really happened to Jim. Why didn't you answer his call?"

Sean stared for a moment and then said, "So you're legit! I thought you were either a telemarketer or some scammer, using Jim's name to get your foot in the door."

I briefly studied him. He was of medium height with a mop of curly dark hair and equally dark, inquisitive eyes. And before

I spoke a word, Melissa said, "Well, now that you know he's on the up and up and can hopefully make things right, you can set up a time for an interview. We had a hard time believing that Jim took opioids, so here's your chance to help Mr. Fox find evidence that he didn't."

Sean looked my way and said, "Sure, but it will have to be much later. I have classes this afternoon."

"Fine by me," I agreed.

He got a text and muttered to himself, "Shit."

"Bad news?" I asked.

"Oh, sorry. I'm just bummed. My golf buddy cancelled on me for tomorrow. We're both free on Thursday mornings and usually play a round of golf. This is not the first time he bailed out at the last moment."

"May I take his place?"

"You're kidding!"

"I'm serious. My clubs are in the trunk of my car."

"Fantastic! We've booked a reservation at the Oak Creek Golf Club. Tee time is at 8:30 in the morning. Do you need directions how to get there?"

"My GPS will find it," I assured him. And I added, "We can kill two birds with one stone."

He stared for a second. Then he seemed to get my meaning and agreed, "That's a deal."

He checked the time and said, "I'd better run. See you tomorrow, Mr. Fox."

He bent down to hug his friend good-bye and was gone. The young man never even sat down.

Melissa said, "I have to be at a lecture hall clear across the campus soon, so I can't stay much longer either. Did you have any more questions?"

"Not that I can think of at the moment."

We walked out of the Anthill Pub & Grille together. Outside, before we went in opposite directions, I promised to let her know of any progress in my investigation.

CHAPTER 11

The good part about being unattached was that I had no accountability to anyone and could make decisions on the spur of the moment. I always kept a set of clubs, golf shoes, and a pair of shorts in the trunk of my Jeep. All that remained for me to do was to search for a reasonably priced hotel in the vicinity. I found one a few miles from the golf course.

I spent the evening in my hotel room. First I tended to my daily stretches as an artificial limb wearer, and then I got busy with the tablet. I had kept notes of what I'd learned from each person interviewed so far, and now added the information obtained from Melissa. I had also jotted down impressions I'd formed about the witnesses, which I now looked over.

Tho Hoàng: *Interesting statement that anything less than an "A" from his son was not acceptable.*

Lan Hoàng: *Her opinion that the overdose had been meant for someone other than Jim is worth for me to consider.*

Jennifer Hoàng: *A feisty young woman who was able to manipulate her brother by counting on his trusting nature. Thinks he committed suicide because of being under pressure to excel.*

Mai Hoàng: *A self-assured old lady who may know more than meets the eye.*

As for Diana Deschamps, the principal of the school, there was no need for notes. My thoughts about her were self-evident.

Nelson Montagu (Mr. Drama): *A passionate man who still keeps in touch to date with former drama student, Mike Higginson.*

Burt Trolley (stage crew member): *Gave me a strange look and seemed uneasy when thinking I was acting on behalf of the police department.*

I added that day's segment about Melissa Van der Molen: *For a spoiled rich girl, she is surprisingly down to earth. Interesting how Sean jumped to attention when summoned by Melissa, who seemed bossy and in charge when he showed up.*

Then I reviewed all the information I'd gathered and reread what people had told about Jim:

His father had said, "He was a good kid." And from the mouth of his mother, "Our Jim gave us nothing but joy, from the time he was born until the end." The sister mentioned that he was gullible and that she thought it paradoxical that such a brain could also be naïve. I remembered her saying, "He was a trusting soul and took everyone's word at face value."

Grandma's words, "No drugs, no drink. Suicide a sin. He good boy!" came to mind. From Diana Deschamps I had learned that, besides excelling academically, Jim had been a nice kid who followed the rules. Mr. Drama tagged him as an exemplary student with leadership ability. And finally, today's entry of Melissa, who admired him for his kindness and honesty. Her statements, "There wasn't a mean bone in his body," and "He didn't even see any bad in others," stayed vivid in my memory.

It was clear that everyone appeared to agree that Jim Hoàng had been a good kid. And what I had learned from today's talk with the young woman confirmed his sister's comment that he had been easy to manipulate. The only contradicting statement, so far, was the stage fright thing. His grandmother said the boy had been plagued by stage fright and Melissa vehemently denied it. It was possible that he kept it a secret from everybody except Mai Hoàng, who appeared to have been his sounding board. Did whether or not he suffered from stage fright even matter in my investigation? Probably not.

The overall image I had gathered of Jim Hoàng thus far was that he'd been a highly intelligent, well-behaved kid going by the rules, generous with sharing his talents, and trusting others to the point of being easy to fool. Everyone I had talked to did not believe he ever took opioids. Could it be that he was a different person beneath that outer shell?

And then there were the facts: He had received news of being accepted to UC Irvine on a full scholarship the very day he took his last breath. He had enjoyed the company of a gorgeous girlfriend and had landed himself one of the lead roles in the school's acclaimed musical, premiering that same night. Was all of that compatible with suicide? Hardly! I considered, what if there was a deep, disturbing secret that lurked underneath all that bliss?

Then again, the ultimate possibility was murder, which Tho and others wanted me to prove. But there has to be a motive for homicide. So far, I hadn't been able to come up with a single one.

Give it a rest, Nick, I told myself, watched the evening news on TV, and then called it a night.

CHAPTER 12

We both showed up at the golf course several minutes before tee time, allowing for checking in at the desk and getting a cart. Sean seemed to be a member and explained that I was taking his buddy's place. The employee gave me a friendly nod and said, "Welcome to Oak Creek Golf Club!" The guest fee was a bit pricy but I figured since I hadn't played golf in over two weeks, I could treat myself to the new experience. We were lucky in that we didn't get teamed up with other people that Thursday morning. Sean picked up a score card and we were set to go.

On the walk over to our assigned cart, Sean asked, "What's your handicap?"

Since I was wearing shorts my condition was in plain view. I stood still and stared him down.

"I meant the golf handicap."

"Oh," I replied, "I haven't established an official one yet, but am guessing it's about 22. What's yours?"

"I'm a 20." Then he pointed at my prosthesis and said, "But I admit that I'm curious. Are you a veteran?"

"No. I used to be a homicide detective of the L. A. County Sheriff's Department before I lost my leg."

"I see. So now you've turned private investigator."

I did not correct him. Let him assume that, I thought.

Once we teed off at the first hole, we concentrated on the game and kept the conversation to a minimum. There was a threesome in front of us, but they hardly slowed us down. It soon became clear that this 18-hole course with its tapered fairways, beautiful lakes, and carved bunkers came with many challenges. Sean, as a regular, was familiar with the layout. I appreciated that, rather than using this to his advantage, he pointed out the difficulties.

For instance, a tee shot with a driver down the left-hand side of the fairway at hole one would have been my choice, since a large bunker made the right side less attractive. But he tipped me off that second shots onto the green from that medium-length par four were better from the right. I followed his advice, and we both parred the first hole.

Hole six was a long par five and a challenge for my ball striking, as a creek twisted its way down an entire side of the fairway, and there were bunkers everywhere. Sure enough, my shot landed in the creek, resulting in a stroke penalty. The good part was that I happened upon a heron, fishing in the winding creek. What a delightful sight!

The easiest was hole eight, a short par four. I chose a fairway wood and my opponent reached for a long iron, and we both had good tee shots between the eucalyptus trees, leaving us with lofted iron shots onto the green. I parred it but Sean ended up with a birdie. We came upon more eucalyptus trees flanking both sides of the fairway at the next hole. Sean remarked that owls and hawks frequently nested in them, but I didn't spot any birds that day.

At one point while driving our cart to the next hole I asked, "How long have you been playing?"

He replied, "My dad started me in elementary school. By the time I was in eighth grade, the two of us played twice a week.

Unfortunately, Dad hurt his back when I was in high school. Even strong painkillers didn't give him enough relief and he had to quit. I stopped playing too and only took it up again recently when starting at UCI." And he asked, "What about you?"

I grinned and said, "For me it worked the other way around. I used to be active in different sports until I got injured. I started picking up golf a little over three years ago."

"Looks like you're a fast learner," he complimented.

By far the most challenging was hole 15, par four. More eucalyptus vegetation bordered the left of the fairway, and an imposing deep bunker guarded the right. My drive landed in the bunker and it took three strokes to get it out of there. On top of that, the green was elevated, and I missed it with a shot to the right that rolled my ball several yards down to the bottom of the hill. My score for that hole was 8. Sean's drive hit the trees but he ended with a slightly better score of a double bogey.

At the end of the round when we added up our scores, we learned that Sean shot a 90. I shot a 95, minus the two strokes because of the difference in handicaps, putting my score at 93.

I said, "I didn't beat you, but 93 is not too shabby for a middle-aged man." And checking the time of 12:35, I added, "We moved along nicely by finishing in a bit over four hours. I'll treat you to lunch; hope you're hungry."

"Like a wolf!" he said.

CHAPTER 13

We lunched at the golf course's Oak Creek Café out on their patio on tasty chicken teriyaki bowls. It was obvious to both of us that the important thing was not the food but our talk.

We were at the last few bites when I started with, "Now Sean, describe what your friend Jim Hoàng was like in one word."

"Loyal," he said, without having to think about it.

"Give me a for instance."

"When he got interested in theater stuff and hung out with Melissa and the drama crowd, he didn't just drop me. We stayed friends and he made time to also hang with me."

"Yes, that took loyalty," I agreed. "Was there anything different about Jim in the days or even weeks before his tragic death?"

"He seemed the same as always," he replied.

"There was nothing that bothered him and he wasn't afraid of anyone?"

"No. I'm sure he would've told me."

"I understand that you were not accepted to this university straight from high school but recently transferred from Pasadena City College."

"I guess Melissa told you. I goofed on the PSAT test in the spring of my junior year. Then I took the SAT in the fall as a senior. That time around I felt lousy with a fever during the test and was diagnosed with mono a day later. So I did poorly again."

I remarked, "Suffering from infectious mononucleosis is a long ordeal. I had my own experience with it." I grinned and added, "But you made it here in the end, so it's all good."

"Actually, I didn't enroll at PCC right after graduating from Citadel. Losing my best friend did a number on me, so I sat a year out from school."

I stuffed the last forkful of food into my mouth, and after swallowing said, "Speaking of Melissa, you like her, don't you?"

"It's that obvious?" He didn't expect a reply and continued, "Her boyfriend is a jerk. I can wait."

"Let's get back to the subject of your friend Jim. Tell me when you last saw him."

I saw pain in his eyes when he answered, "I came to see him perform at opening night of *Woeful*."

"I meant before. Did you talk to him that day?"

He nodded. Then, trying hard not to fall apart, he told his story: "My parents were out of town and I'd received the UCI rejection on that Saturday. I felt sorry for myself and pinched my dad's beer. I was on my second bottle when Jim came by, all happy about being accepted. When he learned of the negative response I'd gotten, he felt truly sad for me. I told him, 'Don't sweat it. This is *your* day. Let's celebrate!' And I urged him to have a bottle of beer. Jim never drank and at first refused, but I insisted until he gave in. I'm sure it was because he felt bad for me."

He took a deep breath. "I'm not proud of having pressured him to have the beer, but he didn't stay long and didn't even finish it. I could tell he hated the taste."

I thought, at least the mystery of the alcohol is solved. Aloud I said, "Why didn't you come forward and tell this to the authorities?"

"Nobody asked me. The police only interviewed kids who were in the drama class and performed in the musical. Besides, I didn't want to advertise that I was occasionally dipping into Dad's liquor." He looked at me sideways and confessed, "I'm glad it's out. I've been feeling guilty all this time."

"As you should."

"Will there be consequences for me?"

I stated, "The case is officially closed. If I find evidence of foul play it could be reopened, but the cause of death was an opioid overdose, not alcohol poisoning. Granted, the beer in his system did not help matters."

Sean looked so dejected that I added, "But I see no reason why I should have to make the source of it public."

"Thank you."

I changed the subject and asked, "Did Jim have any enemies?"

"We were on a debate team together and things could get heated and nasty at times with the opposing team, but I wouldn't have called them enemies. Overall, Jim was well-liked. People might have been a little jealous because he was so smart and had it all together, but nobody hated him."

"I've asked you this before, but are you sure there was nothing that he worried about or had a conflict with in the days prior to his passing?"

"Not that I was aware of."

I probed, "We've established that your friend - - with the exception of his last day - - never drank alcohol. What about drugs, illegal or prescription?"

"I am 100 percent sure that he didn't do either," Sean maintained.

"Besides you and Melissa, can you think of anyone else he would have confided in?"

He thought about it and then said, "Maybe his grandma. I was at his house a lot in the four years of high school and noticed that he was close to her."

"What's your opinion of his sister?"

"I haven't seen her lately, but in those days Jennifer was rebellious. Jim was in charge of her while the parents minded the store, but she defied him any chance she got." He laughed and added, "Jim didn't even realize what she got away with, he was such a trusting soul."

I could not think of anything else to ask him and concluded the interview, giving him my number in case he should later remember something that might help me.

I stayed at the Oak Creek Café's patio a bit longer, typing a summary of the conversation we'd had onto my tablet while everything was still fresh in my memory. In the personal note I was in the habit of adding to each person interviewed, I now wrote, Sean Brooks: *The remark he made about Melissa's current boyfriend being a jerk and that he himself could wait was an indication that he'd loved her for years. The mystery of alcohol showing in Jim's autopsy results, when he apparently did not drink, is now solved.*

CHAPTER 14

On Friday, November 16, several people got in touch with me. Tho called, wanting to know how the investigation was coming along. I pacified him as much as I could. Diana Deschamps sent me the following text, "*I do recall something about a student who performed in Woeful that might help you.*" I texted her back and we arranged to meet at a Starbuck's in Pasadena the next afternoon, Saturday. I also got a call from Sean Brooks and our conversation went as follows:

"Hi, Mr. Fox. You said to let you know if I remembered anything that could've bothered Jim. I thought of something last night."

"Shoot!"

"About two weeks before he died, he witnessed something disturbing involving an adult and a student."

"He told you that?"

"Yeah, but he wasn't sure whether what he saw was actually what it looked like."

"Was he talking about something of a sexual nature?"

"I think so, but he was not specific."

"What exactly did he say?"

"That he saw a person of authority and a student in an inappropriate situation. When I asked him for particulars, he wouldn't go into details or give away any names, since he wasn't sure if he had jumped to the wrong conclusion."

I asked, "What he saw happened at the Citadel High School?"

"Yeah, but he didn't say whether it was a teacher, just a person in power. I could tell that he was burdened by what he saw and didn't know what to do. My advice was to notify his counselor or even the principal, but he didn't want to get anyone into trouble in case he was wrong about the whole thing."

"So he kept quiet?" I asked.

"I don't think he informed anyone, but he may have gone directly to the persons involved, either the adult or the student, so they could vindicate themselves."

"This gives me food for thought. Thanks for letting me know," I said, and we ended the call.

I thought about the alleged inappropriate situation that Jim may have witnessed for a long time. It could have been any adult on the school premises; from the janitor all the way up to the principal, but I had the feeling that Sean assumed it was a teacher. And by the sheer percentage of persons in authority at a high school campus, the odds pointed to a teacher. Of course, there might have been an innocent explanation to what Jim had witnessed. In that case, I was wasting my time dwelling on it.

In the evening I received a bombshell of a call. I usually let my son call me at his convenience, not the other way around. News from him was overdue, so when I recognized the number I picked up and said, "Hi there, Connor, how's it going?" To my surprise it was my ex's voice I heard, saying, "It's me and it's not going well. Connor has been acting up, and since you're his father, I thought you should know."

"What do you mean by 'acting up'?"

"He's been hanging with the wrong group of friends and we're putting a stop to it. It turns out that he's ditched many times, and partied with his despicable buddies - - most of them drop-outs - - instead of going to school."

"Is he addicted to illegal drugs?" I asked.

"Hopefully not, but he's been experimenting with several of them and also alcohol, we've learned."

"How long has this been going on?"

"For quite some time, but we only got wise to it three weeks ago when he got arrested because his scum friends were caught stealing iPhones from a store."

"Wait a minute," I said, "if he was arrested, he must have taken part in the crime."

"Well, he was there with them but didn't realize what they were up to. The charges against him were later dropped. It's a long story, and I don't want to go into it right now."

And without giving me further details, she went on, "The most important thing is to get him away from the bad kids he's been friends with. We've been looking into sending him to a tough love camp and found one with a reputation of excellent results."

"I see. How is he reacting to that?"

"He didn't want to go but had no choice. It's a six-month commitment."

"Are you telling me he's already at the camp and I can't talk to him?"

"Yes, we drove him there this morning. It's only a two-hour drive from our house."

"This is coming out of the blue. I have a hard time adjusting to the idea."

"It's not easy for me either."

I asked, "Is he permitted to go home for Christmas?"

She sounded close to tears when she answered, "I don't think so."

After a pause she said, "When his time at the facility comes to an end in the spring, it will be crucial that he doesn't go back to the same group of pals that got him into trouble. Would you be willing to have him come live with you in the summer and maybe even enroll for his senior high school year near you in Southern California?"

I was speechless.

After a long pause she said, "You have plenty of time to think things over. It doesn't have to be decided for a few months. But you *are* his father, and it is only fair that you should share responsibility."

I didn't sleep well on that Friday night. The problem with Connor weighed heavily on my mind. And it looked like it was going to be *my* problem. The thing about "sharing responsibility" that my ex had tossed my way irked me. She had moved far away when my son was seven years old and for ten years never batted an eye as to being solely responsible for him. Now, at the first sign of trouble, she wanted me to step back into the picture. I thought, but the fact remains, I am his dad. So much for staying "unattached."

CHAPTER 15

Ms. Deschamps and I drove into the Starbucks parking area seconds apart. I was right behind her when she walked toward the entrance. Clad in jeans and flats, the private school principal made a different impression than in the business suit and heels I had seen her wearing last time. She looked sexy to me.

"Wait up!" I called out.

She turned her head and there were those striking green eyes again.

Settled with our fancy coffee beverages, we got straight down to business.

She said, "The student I was referring to in my text was Alex Topalian, and I wanted to let you know that he has an eidetic memory."

"What does that mean?"

"Having an eidetic memory is the ability to recall images with accuracy. People often call it a photographic memory, but that term is incorrect."

"Thanks for the heads up," I said. "He may recall something that'll help with my task. I already have him on my list of people to interview."

I later realized that she could have simply told me this with a phone call or sent a text. So the feeling was mutual; the woman had wanted to see me just as much as I had longed for a meeting in person. To my delight, the two of us felt comfortable with one another. We chatted at length on that Saturday afternoon, and it had nothing to do with Jim Hoàng.

She first said, "Something is troubling you." Which made me tell her about my ex-wife's phone call of the previous night and all that it entailed.

She heard me out and then remarked, "I hope they'll do a good job at that camp to get your son back on track. And come summertime, you might both benefit from having him live with you."

Then she got a faraway look in her eyes and stated, "I'd give anything to have my own child back, even if it meant dealing with a drug problem and other issues."

I gently asked, "What happened to your kid?"

And so I learned that her son - - who would have been in eighth grade by that time - - had died two years previously after a long battle with leukemia. She shared her experience of taking her boy in and out of hospitals and doctors' appointments for several years. Her renewed hopes when he was in remission, followed by the big letdowns as his illness kept coming back, threw her into an emotional rollercoaster. In the end, there was nothing any doctor or hospital could do for her son.

A death of a child can either draw a couple closer together or pull them apart. The relationship with her husband after their son's passing went from bad to worse, ending in divorce in March of the current year.

Our discussion suddenly changed back to me when she inquired into my disability. To my astonishment, I told it all in gory detail: The sabotaging of my car ending in an explosion with me in it. Waking up in the hospital to find out I'd lost a kidney and my left leg. My decision to take early retirement rather than sit at a desk job, and finally, how I coped with my artificial limb from day to day. This was the first time I had discussed all this at length with anyone, and a woman at that.

She listened with keen attention, asking a question here and there with a matter-of-fact attitude. I sensed that she cared, but to her credit, she did not make any pitying comments. I had not felt this much at ease with any female for years.

Our coffee cups had long stood empty and people at tables around us had come and gone when she suggested, "Since we've shared so much personal info, I suggest we graduate to first names. Don't you think, Nick?"

"Okay by me, Diana!"

Before we parted I inquired, "Would you like to go out sometime?"

"You bet," she replied.

On my drive home I thought, I haven't been interested in dating for ages. What the hell happened to me?

CHAPTER 16

The next former student of Citadel High School on my agenda was Mike Higginson. I had an appointment to meet him at his apartment in Westwood at 4:30 p.m. on Tuesday, November 20. Traffic was horrendous and I got there ten minutes late.

He met my apologies with a smile and said, "No worries," ushering me into a spacious living room to have a seat. He added, "I'm in the process of brewing myself a cup of tea. May I bring you one too, or would you prefer a different beverage?"

"Just water would be great," I said.

I sidestepped the large beige leather sofa and sat down on the matching leather chair. While he went to the kitchen, I glanced around the room. There was a big screen TV against the wall I was facing, flanked by a credenza on one side and a bookcase on the other. At the far end of the room stood an upright piano. The prints hanging on the walls were ultra-modern. Everything was neat and tidy. With the exception of a large framed photo of my host holding hands with another man, there were no knickknacks.

Mike came back into the room carrying a tray with his tea, my water, a little dish with what looked like fancy crackers, and paper napkins. As he arranged the items on the glass-top coffee table, I got a chance to study him. He was a handsome blond, light-eyed young man, and his movements were graceful as he sat our drinks down on coasters.

I said, "You have a real nice place here, and it's in walking distance of UCLA; what a bonus."

"Thanks, but it's not only mine. I share the condominium with my boyfriend." And he beamed and announced, "We got engaged last weekend!"

"Congratulations! No wonder you're full of smiles. When you first opened the door to me I thought, *here is an extremely happy man.*"

He thrust both arms high up as if he were on stage and proclaimed, "Isn't it marvelous that same-sex marriage became legal?" His question was rhetorical and he continued, "No more games of hide and seek. We are equals!"

I pointed to the picture on the credenza and remarked, "That dark-haired man must be your fiancé. Is he also a student at the university?"

"Oh no, he's past getting an education and has already made a name for himself as a fashion designer. You may have heard of him, he goes by Salvadore."

"Sorry, I don't know anything about the fashion industry. And I admit that I hardly know more of the drama and theater arts, which I understand you're planning to major in."

He took a sip of his tea and then said, "You're well informed. My guess is that Nelson told you that I'm pursuing a future in the performing arts." My momentary blank stare prompted him to add, "Nelson Montagu, that is. Back in high school I called him Mr. Drama but I've since graduated to addressing him by first name."

"So you keep in touch?"

"Absolutely. I look to him as my mentor. And by the way, he gave me a heads-up about you last week, so I was expecting to hear from you."

"Okay then, let's cut to the chase. Tell me about Jim Hoàng. What did you think of him?"

"I didn't know him well. He only joined the drama class in our senior year. He was a brain, a nice guy, and straight. I didn't have any other classes with him. Of course we rehearsed together for the musical *Woeful*. Melissa, Jim, and I sang a trio in the second act. As I remember, on that opening night, Jim was spot on. We all were."

"Did he show any sign of stage fright before the performance, though?"

"Not that I was aware."

"Did you notice anything different about Jim either before or during his act that night?"

He seemed to think about it and then stated, "No, I can't say that I did. But you should ask Melissa about that. He was mostly hanging with her before the show and during intermission. Maybe she remembers something."

I looked him straight in the eye and asked, "What's your opinion of why he died?"

He blinked and said, "Is there a dispute about the cause of death?"

"He expired due to an opioid overdose, that's unquestionable. What I meant is, do you believe that he was a user and accidentally overdosed, or committed suicide, or that we may be looking at a homicide?"

The young man slowly drank some more tea before answering, "That's a tough question. I don't think he was the type to regularly take opioids, nor would I have believed he was suicidal. That leaves your third suggestion, but I can't imagine that anyone would have wanted to murder him."

And with a charming smile he added, "That puts a dent into your task, doesn't it?"

"He was well liked?" I asked.

"As I mentioned before, I didn't know him well, but as far as I could tell, nobody held a grudge, at least not anyone at Citadel drama."

No further questions came to mind, so I downed the rest of my water, thanked him for his time, and got up to leave.

At home I entered that day's interview to my records, adding the following personal note, Mike Higginson: *Is on first name basis with his former drama teacher. This could be significant or may mean nothing at all.*

CHAPTER 17

Like most years in the last decade, I was invited to spend Thanksgiving with the family of my former Sheriff's department partner, Rick. He lived in an unpretentious Spanish-style home in a small town in the San Fernando Valley. When I got there at one o'clock in the afternoon and rang the doorbell, I heard Norma, his wife, yell through the open kitchen window, "The door is open, come on in."

I followed the smell of roasting turkey and found Norma, assisted by her mother, tending to things on the stove. I gave both ladies the obligatory hug and set my two bottles of Chardonnay on the counter.

Norma shooed me out of the kitchen, saying, "Make yourself at home, Nick. I believe everyone is in the yard. We'll eat in less than an hour."

Stepping out the back door, I didn't need to be introduced to anyone. Years of gatherings with Rick's family had made me familiar with them all. I stood still and watched the activities in progress. Rick's kids, both girls, were engaged in a game of backyard bocce ball against their two teenage male cousins. His sister and brother-in-law slammed one another in a fierce ping-pong match, and my friend himself played darts with Norma's father. The two family cats, Salt and Pepper, where in hiding. Too much commotion for their taste, I imagined.

One of the girls spotted me and yelled, "Uncle Nick is here!" And she quickly came over to give me a hug before going back to her game. My ex-partner's kids had called me "Uncle" from the time they were toddlers and now, at ages 14 and 12, there was no reason to change the tradition.

Rick beckoned me to the dart board, shoved his three darts into my hand, and suggested I take over the game in progress against his father-in-law, while he checked if he was needed in the kitchen. I looked at the scores: His opponent had closed the numbers 20, 17, 15, and the bull's eye, and had accumulated a score of 137. Rick had closed the 19s, 18s, and 16s, and only had 104 points.

I teased, "So you rely on me to fix your goof-ups! I'll try, but there's no guarantee of success," and cheerfully took over.

I managed to make some more points but never closed the bull's eye. Norma's dad was a precise shot. He ended up closing all numbers, winning the game with a final score of 197 to my 173. He patted me on the shoulder and remarked, "That goes to show you that age is not a disadvantage in dart throwing."

When the turkey was out of the oven and needed to sit for a while, Norma called out to her girls to help set the table. Minutes later, we all flocked to the dining room, where Rick carved the bird while his wife and mother-in-law carried in the mashed potatoes, gravy, yams, green beans, stuffing, and cranberries. I made myself useful and opened a bottle of chardonnay. Rick's brother-in-law, a minister, led us in saying grace so the feast could begin.

Initially, we concentrated on eating but soon the conversations started to flow. The youngsters held their own chatter at the far end of the table. As for the adult topics, we discussed anything from family camping trips and world cruises, electric cars, latest movies and plays, to finicky appetites of pets. Speaking of which, likely due to the smell of turkey, Pepper soon made an appearance, followed by Salt. The only subjects avoided were shop talk and politics. Norma had strict rules and tolerated neither at the dinner table.

I observed the family members drawn together in perfect harmony and listened to their humorous banter with a touch of envy. And not for the first time I became aware of the well-balanced relationship between Rick and Norma. Their jobs - - his as a homicide detective and hers as a forensic technician - - were interwoven at times. But Norma made sure that their home life didn't suffer under the strain of solving crimes.

At the end of the main course we decided to go for a walk around the neighborhood before indulging in apple and pumpkin pies.

CHAPTER 18

We went in small clusters, each with its own topic of conversation. The girls and their cousins walked, or practically ran, ahead of everyone. They were followed by the three women: Norma, her mother, and sister-in-law. Rick's male in-laws were engaged in football talk, oblivious to anyone else, and my friend and I brought up the rear.

"So Fox," he said, "How's your love life?"

"Nonexistent, but you'll be the first to know of any change."

"And how's your memoir coming along?"

"True crime short stories," I corrected. "I've been too busy to write lately."

"Ah yes, you've been meddling in private eye stuff. Is that why you're so glum?"

"I haven't made much progress but that's not why I'm bummed." And I told him about Connor.

He stated, "Those things don't happen from one day to the next. You were unaware of red flags prior to your ex-wife's call?"

"I had no idea!" And I thought back to what my son had let slip about his stepsisters in phone conversations over the last few months and said, "My ex must have been too busy grooming the twins - - one is into figure skating, the other ballet - - to pay attention to Connor. My guess is that he resented it. That doesn't excuse his behavior, though."

I continued, "The last time I saw Connor in person was almost a year ago, between Christmas and New Year's. I didn't notice any warning signs then."

My friend said, "Enrolling him in that tough love camp was most likely a good thing. He may be rebellious at first, but those places can do wonders to get teens out of trouble. And come spring, if you decide to have him live with you, Norma and I will support you all the way."

"Thanks," I gasped, slightly out of breath. We had been walking uphill for a bit and he suddenly realized it and slowed down for me.

Once we were on level ground and I was stabilized, he asked, "Want to tell me about your sleuthing?" So I did, going into details of each person interviewed so far.

He listened carefully, never interrupting, until my narrative came to an end. Then he said, "Everyone seems to agree that your victim was not an opioid user, and according to people's statements and the fact that he got a full scholarship to UCI on the very day he died, it's unlikely that he was suicidal. That leaves homicide. But there appears to be no motive for murder, at least not on the surface. He was well liked with apparently no enemies, a crime of passion is unlikely, and greed doesn't come into play since he was a poor kid. The only other possibility that comes to mind would be if he knew someone's dark secret and needed to be silenced."

I had long come to the same conclusions and commented, "Or if he himself was involved in the secret and was ready to confess."

We stayed silent for about half a block. I spotted his father-in-law and brother-in-law ahead of us, turning down a side street as he continued, "It takes two to three hours until the deadly effect of an opioid overdose manifests itself. So as far as suspects go, we're looking at the people who were close enough to your victim during that time to slip pills into his food or drink."

I nodded and said, "That would be the cast of the musical *Woeful* and the stage crew members - - all drama students of Citadel High School - - plus their drama teacher as director. There was a professional choreographer, but since he or she was an outsider and hadn't known Jim prior to putting on the musical, we can disregard that person."

"Tell me about the girlfriend, I believe Melissa is her name. What did you think of her?"

I stated, "She's maybe a bit bossy, but otherwise I had a good impression. Apparently, she had been heartbroken after Jim's death and had even seen a psychologist to help her over the grief."

Rick smirked and remarked, "You can take that with a grain of salt. Teenagers, especially the ones into theater, can be melodramatic. She sounds well-adjusted by now, and like you mentioned, has a new boyfriend."

Then he said, "Go over for me one more time what the victim's friend - - the one not in the drama class - - said about something that Jim had witnessed between a teacher and student."

"That would be Sean Brooks. He was actually vague about it and - -"

"Who was vague? Sean or the victim?"

"Sean said that Jim had been vague." And I went on, "I have it all written down but of course don't have my notes on me."

"Try to remember as best you can."

I rehashed the phone conversation with Sean in my mind and then said, "Okay, this is what I recall. Jim confided in Sean that he had witnessed a person of authority and a student in an inappropriate situation. As I said, Jim was vague with what he told Sean, not giving any names or going into details, since he wasn't sure of what he saw. The only straightforward fact Jim divulged to his friend was that the incident happened at the Citadel High School. When Sean advised him to notify his counselor or go to the principal, Jim stated that he didn't want to get anyone in trouble in case he had jumped to the wrong conclusion."

"I see. That *is* vague. And we're not even sure that a teacher was involved, since the kid said "a person of authority.""

"Exactly. It could have been anyone, from the janitor all the way up to the principal herself."

"When you told me about the interview with the head of school, you only referred to the person as the principal. So it's a woman?" Rick asked.

I hoped that he kept looking straight ahead and not at me as I replied, "Yep. With striking green eyes."

There was a knowing tone in his voice as he stated, "But you don't think for a minute that she was involved in this inappropriate situation with a student."

"Nope."

He changed direction in his analysis and said, "Interesting how the victim's sister believes that it was a suicide. You know the father personally. Do you think it's possible that he put that much pressure on his son?"

"It's true that he expected excellence from him, but it is also clear that learning came easy to Jim, who seemed to effortlessly get straight A's."

"What do you think of the mother's theory that the pills were meant for someone else and her son accidentally swallowed them in food or drink?"

"That is farfetched but not impossible," I commented.

"Too bad that there was a bit of a language barrier with the grandmother. I have the feeling that she could have told you more, if she'd wanted to."

"You may be right."

Rick then stated, "After all the years you spent on the force I don't have to tell you that some, or perhaps all, of your witnesses may have been lying."

"I'm aware of that." And I added, "In the back of my mind I know that I missed something. Someone told me a crucial piece of information but it escapes me for the moment."

"Give it time. It will pop into your head when least expected."

I sighed and admitted, "I should be further along with my investigation by now but am still feeling my way in the dark."

"You have more suspects to be interviewed, correct?"

"Just a few. Two more former students of Citadel High School who were performing in the musical, and a next-door-neighbor kid who was friends with Jim since Kindergarten."

"You'll get there in the end," he assured me, full of confidence.

"I'm not so sure. Do you suppose I could seek out Sergeant Anna Diego, the main investigating detective of the closed case, and compare notes if I get into a bind?"

"There's no law that forbids it," he said with a chuckle.

I had been so concentrated on our talk that I hadn't realized we had gone full circle until we stood in front of Rick's house. Everyone else had obviously made it back minutes earlier.

He checked his watch and said, "Just in time for pie and NFL football. Should be interesting to watch the Washington Redskins and the Dallas Cowboys going at it."

CHAPTER 19

Alex Topalian, who attended a Northern California university, was home for the Thanksgiving holiday weekend. He had promised to shoot baskets with his younger brother and friends during his visit and decided to combine it with my interview. He suggested that we should have our talk on Black Friday in the afternoon, while he was at a park with the kids. It wasn't ideal, but I took him up on it since he had plans for every day during his short visit home.

We agreed to meet at Two Strike Park in his La Crescenta neighborhood at two o'clock, near the basketball court. Once in town, I drove many blocks up the hill to reach the park above Foothill Boulevard, nestled below the mountain range. I parked alongside Rosemont Avenue and, realizing that I was early, first had a look around.

At the topmost part of the playground was a field, serving both soccer and softball. There were no games or practices held at the time, just a few kids kicking a ball around. In fact, the entire park was not crowded at all. I assumed that people were out shopping. I walked by the rock climbing zone where youngsters could test their agility with ropes. Canopies covered the playground equipment area to protect children from the burning sun on slides and the like. To the right of the swings, there was a huge grassy area where dogs and kids had a free run. I spotted picnic benches and tables, most of them in the shade of trees. At the lower edge of the park was a memorial with engraved names of local veterans who had lost their lives in combat. I stood in front of it for a few moments. Although I did not know any of the honored soldiers personally, they deserved my respect. And then it was time to head over to the basketball court.

It looked like Alex Topalian and his entourage were already there; I saw an adult and five boys, possibly of middle school age, shooting baskets. There was a towhead among the bunch, and the other boys had dark hair, including the young adult. Nobody paid attention to me, so I sat down on a nearby bench in the shade of an oak tree and watched the action on the basketball court.

They had apparently formed teams of three players each, and it looked like they knew their stuff. Both sides made several baskets with bank shots, but I noticed a couple of swishes too. The tallest of the dark-haired kids even landed an alley-oop, dunking the ball into the hoop. The youngsters were good at defense too, blocking many shots. One kid made a fast break by advancing the ball and scoring after a great steal.

Even though the adult among them was a team player, and no doubt good at it, he didn't hog the ball and acted more like a coach. He suddenly checked his watch, then looked around and spotted me. He said something to the kids - - I was too far away to make out his words - - and they continued the game without him.

CHAPTER 20

Alex Topalian came over to me, asking, "Mr. Fox?" I nodded. We shook hands and he sat down next to me, making sure he had a clear view of the basketball court.

I observed, "You must drive a van to accommodate all those kids."

"My little brother and his friends all live in the neighborhood. We walked over."

I pointed to the tallest one on the court, who was dribbling the ball at the moment, and remarked, "That boy is your brother, correct?"

He smiled and said, "An easy pick for you since we look alike."

"Is he by chance following in your footsteps as a student of Citadel High School?"

"Right now he's attending an Armenian middle school, but our parents may enroll him at Citadel for his high school years. They haven't made up their minds yet."

I felt it was time to get down to business and said, "Your seeing me on a holiday weekend is appreciated."

"When you first contacted me, I wasn't too keen to talk with you. The idea of rehashing what happened to Jim didn't seem necessary. But when you said that there might be a possibility of foul play, I changed my mind. If you can prove that he was murdered, the culprit needs to be put to justice."

I thought, I couldn't have put it any better myself. Aloud I said, "Okay, tell me your relationship to Jim."

"We had both attended Citadel all through high school. Earlier, he was in my English class, and in our senior year he took drama, which I had been enrolled in all along. I can't say that we were best friends, but he definitely was my buddy, at least the last year in drama. He landed himself the lead role of Peterus in the musical *Woeful,* and I was his understudy."

"How did that come about?" I wanted to know.

"It's a simple process. We both auditioned for the part and he got it. I'll admit, he had the better voice, but my acting was superior. Since this was a musical, the better singer won. Mr. Drama gave me a minor role, but I rehearsed the solo parts of Peterus as Jim's understudy."

"I understand that you have an eidetic memory."

The young man looked astonished and said, "How did you discover that? It wasn't in any police report as I'm sure I never mentioned it to the female cop who questioned me."

"The school principal, Ms. Deschamps, volunteered the information."

"Good old Ms. Deschamps!" he cried out. "What else did she say about me?"

"Not a thing. Getting back to your eidetic memory, you must recall things that escape the average person."

He admitted, "It comes in handy when studying. I find it easy to learn things by heart, and in the days that I used to be in plays and musicals, memorizing my lines was a cinch. On the other hand, there are things I'd rather forget, but can't."

I sensed that he wished he hadn't mentioned that last bit and I went with it, asking, "Is there something to do with Jim that you'd rather forget?"

After a long, uncomfortable pause he stated, "I felt bad at the time, and still feel bad now, because during the dress rehearsal on that Saturday morning I jokingly said to him, 'I hope you get sick or drop dead so that I'll get your part.' He laughed and gave me a thumbs up. But then when he literally dropped dead out of the blue, I wished I could have taken those words back."

I changed the subject and said, "Your excellent memory may help with my investigation. Who was close to Jim during the dinner provided for the cast on that Saturday evening before the premiere of *Woeful*?"

He replied, "Melissa was always right next to him, and people came by to chat. There was Mike, Andrew, and me. Also - -"

I interrupted, "Would that be Mike Higginson and Andrew Baldoni?"

"You got it." He continued, "Mr. Drama came over to our group, giving us some last-minute pointers. There was a ninth grade kid who was part of the stage crew, can't think of his name right now - -"

"Burt Trolley?"

"Yes, him. You sure don't miss a beat. Anyhow, Burt rushed over, showing a piece of paper he'd found on the stage floor after the dress rehearsal, asking if it belonged to any of us. It looked like notes, or possibly lines that somebody had jotted down, but none of us claimed it. Some other people walked by throughout dinner, but no one stayed and chatted."

He looked me in the eye and stated, "And for the record, I didn't see anybody tampering with Jim's food or drink, and it sure wasn't me."

He suddenly yelled at one of the boys on the court, "That's a double dribble! Take a penalty turnover."

When his attention turned back to me I said, "Were you aware of Jim's stage fright?"

"No, that's news to me."

"What can you tell me about Melissa?"

"She was Jim's girlfriend, but you must know that already. It was obvious that she was running him."

"How do you mean?"

"All she had to do is snap her little fingers and he jumped to attention. He wasn't the only one, most straight guys in drama had the hots for her."

"Including you?"

"She wasn't my type." And he said, "Oh, I forgot to mention, there was another girl hanging with Jim and eating pizza. I'd never seen her on campus before and he didn't introduce her. I think he smuggled her in just to have dinner with us. She may have been a stepsister or something. Anyhow, she didn't stick around for long. Next time I looked over toward Jim and Melissa, she was gone."

"What made you think of a stepsister?"

"She couldn't have been his real sister since she wasn't Asian."

"I see. Is there anything you remember about Jim or any of the other cast members either on or backstage during that night's show that struck you as unusual?"

He thought about it and then said, "I had only a minor part and was seldom together on stage with Jim, but I noticed that he drank lots of water. I saw him at the water fountain backstage some minutes before show time, again shortly before the first act, and a third time during intermission. I remember thinking that he must have been extremely thirsty. Other than that, I can't recall anything out of the ordinary about Jim.

"And as for the others, everyone was excited about opening night: Melissa was a chatterbox full of anticipation. Andrew kept quiet, probably rehearsing his lines and solo songs in his mind. Mike acted like a fussy mother hen, making sure everyone had their costumes at the ready. And me, although I was the only one with a few speaking lines of the entire cast of townspeople, I was envisioning how I could make myself stand out from the rest when singing in the chorus."

He grinned and added, "Nothing unusual about all that."

That concluded the interview and he went back to his charge on the basketball court.

CHAPTER 21

In my car and homeward bound, I deliberately did not listen to music but mulled over what I had learned from Alex Topalian. He told me a lot but was any of it helpful, I wondered. According to him, the people who had gathered around Jim at his last meal were Melissa, Mike Higginson, Andrew Baldoni, the stage crew kid, Mr. Drama, and Alex Topalian himself. In short, the drama crowd I had already interviewed.

There was this mystery girl who had appeared out of nowhere and as quickly disappeared again. Who was she, and would learning her identity help with the investigation? If she existed and Alex had told the truth - - I saw no reason why he would have made her up - - she was near Jim during his last meal, which meant that I had to add her to my list of suspects.

And there was his mention of having seen Jim at the water fountain numerous times, which struck me as a strange thing for Alex to point out. Should I attach significance to it, or could it be that the pizza Jim ate had simply made him thirsty?

I found it interesting that Alex, unlike most other students, had not been impressed with Melissa. In fact, he gave off the impression that he had disliked her. The incident he had let slip about telling Jim he wished he'd drop dead was downright eerie. Or was it not a slip at all, and he mentioned it to cover himself in case his remark had been overheard by a third party? If so, he had to assume that I was already aware of it.

There were so many other points in that day's discussion that needed to be addressed. For instance, what about that piece of paper that the stage crew kid had found lying around? Should I put any importance to it or was it just a note that someone had accidentally dropped? I couldn't wait to get home to add all this information to my notes.

And then I thought about my next move. The only former Citadel student left to consult was Andrew Baldoni, and he happened to attend a university on the East Coast at the moment. I had no desire to fly over there, where they were experiencing the first snowstorm of the season. According to his parents, he was due to come home for Christmas break. My choices amounted to waiting three weeks to interview him in person or have a phone or skype session within the next few days.

There was the next-door-neighbor girl who'd been friends with Jim since Kindergarten. I decided to tackle her first. Maybe she'd turn out to be a useful source. She had not previously been questioned by the authorities, so her account would be new.

With that settled in my mind, I turned on the radio and listened to classic rock.

CHAPTER 22

My date - - of sorts - - with Diana took place on Sunday, November 25, which was still part of the Thanksgiving weekend. She had agreed to go out to dinner with me, but there was a catch. She volunteered every Sunday afternoon at the Children's Hospital and had asked me to have a short "show and tell" about my disability with what she called her "little troopers." The way she had put it, "It would benefit the children if shown that one could overcome any hardship."

I was reluctant at first as the idea of making a spectacle of myself didn't sit well. But it looked like if I refused, she wasn't going to spend time with me any day soon. Her scheduled volunteer work was from 1:00 to 4:00 and I agreed to show up around 3:30.

Minutes early, I stood at the entrance to the hospital playroom, looking in. Diana sat cross-legged on a rug in the center of the room, surrounded by a flock of small patients. She had one arm wrapped around a little girl with a bandaged eye, the other holding a book from which she read to them. Many of the children were bald, obviously due to chemo treatments, and some sat in wheelchairs. All seemed fascinated with the story about a boy and an elephant that was read to them. Nobody noticed me.

Diana got to the end of the tale, closed the book, and to my amazement there followed a discussion of its content. Like a mini-book club, I silently joked to myself. The kids addressed her as "Dede," which was rather endearing.

She suddenly looked my way, motioned me in, and announced to the kids, "We have Mr. Fox with us today. He lost his leg and has a prosthetic one instead." And when I rolled up my trouser leg and walked around the room, she continued, "As you can see, it functions as his own."

I told them about the physical therapy I had endured as a new artificial limb wearer, and showed them the daily stretches I was still doing. I had hoped that would wrap up what was required of me, but I was wrong. Now the kids' questions began.

One little girl asked, "Does it hurt?"

"Not much anymore," I replied, and the Q & A went on:

"Can you run?"

"Yes, but not as fast as before."

"Can you get it wet and go swimming?"

"My prosthetic leg is sensitive to moisture, so I take it off when showering, but I have a waterproof cover if I want to go swimming."

"Did you need chemo?" a small, bald boy asked.

"No, but I also lost a kidney and needed lots of medication."

"There is something wrong with my kidneys too," a girl in a wheelchair remarked.

"How did you lose your own leg?"

"I used to be a policeman and lost it in the line of duty."

A plucky boy who looked about six years old said, "So a bad guy shot your leg off?"

"No. It happened in an explosion."

"That's worse," the same boy stated. "You didn't even see who did it."

After answering a few more questions, I was relieved when Diana checked the time and said, "It's four o'clock, children. We have to go; see you next Sunday."

"Bye Dede! Bye Mr. Fox!" they called out in unison as a couple of nurses came to fetch them.

Out in the hallway I said, "What brave little warriors those sick kids are!"

"They sure are, and I'm quite attached to them." Then she said, "I'm going to Forest Lawn in Glendale first, it's too early for dinner anyway. I'll meet you later at the restaurant."

"To visit your son's grave?"

She nodded.

"May I join you?"

She seemed shocked for a second, then agreed, "Sure. Why not?"

After a quick stop at the hospital's gift shop, where she bought a bouquet of flowers, we walked to our respective cars in the parking structure and then caravanned to Forest Lawn.

CHAPTER 23

Never having had cause to visit the cemetery, Forest Lawn blew me away. The place was vast with wide open lawns, gardens, a collection of art and historic architecture, several churches, and a museum. Scattered among all that were grave plots, memorial properties, and urn niches. Several roads looped around the enormous place. I followed Diana in her Lexus as she led the way through a labyrinth of streets. We finally climbed around an uphill arc and ended on top of the world, it appeared. She stopped and parked her car on the side of the road, and I did likewise with my older model Jeep Cherokee.

The view down to the city of Glendale and the greater Los Angeles area was breathtaking from that elevation. We both stepped out of our vehicles and admired it. Then we walked along a grassy area, passing marked graves. Diana stopped by a simple commemoration plaque with her son's name, dates of birth and death, and the inscription: *Rest in peace, our brave, young hero.* She placed the flowers by the plate, then stood and bowed her head in what might have been prayer or reverence. I noticed a lone tear roll down her cheek and gave her some privacy by stepping aside.

I passed the time by checking out inscriptions on other plaques nearby. Some were rather funny. There was one that read, *See you soon*, another, *Say hello to Dad*, yet another, *A life and death well done*. I slowly made my way back to where Diana's son was laid to rest. She looked up and made an attempt at a smile.

I asked, "How often do you come here?"

"Every Sunday and if possible once more during the week."

I said, "Your wound is still fresh. It'll get better with time."

"Maybe," she said. "It goes against nature. Children should bury their parents, not the other way around."

I took her hand and squeezed it in understanding. She suddenly shook herself, like a dog coming out of water, and then said, "Let's go."

While walking to where our cars were parked, she checked the time and remarked, "Too bad it's already minutes past five o' clock. The museum exhibits at the hall of the crucifixion and resurrection only go until four. Have you seen them?"

"Actually, this is my first time at Glendale's Forest Lawn, but I've heard of the famous collection."

"You should make a point of coming back here earlier someday, they're a must-see. And located in the mausoleum is a brilliant stained glass re-creation of Da Vinci's painting of the last supper. The sheer size of it takes one's breath away. I believe that viewing closes at 4:30, so we're also too late to see it."

CHAPTER 24

The official date took place at an excellent Chinese restaurant in the Montrose area. The food - - kung pao chicken for her and mu shu shrimp for me - - was excellent and the company even better. We felt comfortable with each other, as if we had been friends for years.

She said, "Thanks for coming to the hospital and showing my little troopers what it's like to live with a prosthetic limb. You did an excellent job and I'm sure the little patients profited from your talk."

"As you know I wasn't keen on doing it, but I'm glad I did. It wasn't really about me at all. When I realized how bravely those sick kids lived their lives, it became all about them." And I added, "You volunteer at that Children's Hospital because of your son. Correct?"

"True. Many volunteers lightened up his life during his ordeal, so it's only right for me to give back."

There was a sudden shift in our conversation when she asked, "So what's the verdict with your investigation into Jim Hoàng's passing?"

"I wish that I could give you a result one way or another, but the truth is that I'm still far away from coming to any conclusion. I've interviewed a slew of people and formed a few ideas, but nothing that sticks. I'm leaning toward foul play, since everything I've learned so far about Jim makes an accidental overdose or suicide highly unlikely. But I have no concrete evidence that it was in fact murder, let alone being able to pinpoint the murderer."

I sighed and went on, "When we first met, I remember you saying during the interview that you made it your business to get to know all the students at Citadel High School personally."

"Yes, I mentioned that and it's true."

"With that in mind, try to think back to that class of three-and-a-half years ago, and tell me if you remember any of his peers or teachers having any kind of issue with Jim."

She thought hard about it, and then said, "There was a bit of an academic competition between another above-average student and Jim, but I doubt that it was anything serious for you to consider."

"Who was the student?"

"Andrew somebody. I can't think of his last name at the moment."

I knew that an Andrew was the last former Citadel student I had on my list to interview but couldn't recall his last name either. I made a mental note to question him about the academic rivalry when the time came.

Diana continued, "I'm sure there was no problem with any of the teachers. As I told you before, Jim was well-behaved and went by the rules. In other words, a model student."

"I'm aware of that."

"So I can't think of anyone that had an issue with him, like you wanted to know. The only thing that comes to mind is that Jim was exceptionally intelligent and excelled at anything he took on. Above all, he had a logical and scientific brain. I was surprised when he enrolled in drama class his senior year and showed an interest in performing in plays and musicals. And most astonishing, it turned out that he had an excellent voice.

"Having said that, I wouldn't be surprised if there had been a certain amount of envy among his fellow students. I mean, he was already known throughout the school as being a brain, and now he excelled at singing to the point of landing a lead part in one of Citadel's prestigious musicals. So a bit of jealousy, yes, but there was certainly no hatred that I could imagine, and I can't narrow it down to any one person."

She shrugged and said, "Sorry! My input wasn't helpful, but it's the best I can do."

"Any kind of information is helpful in the end," I stated.

By the time the waiter brought our fortune cookies, our talk had moved to general matters that people on first dates tend to chat about: best enjoyed foods, excellent movies and plays, favorite types of music, and so forth. The one subject we both avoided was our ex-spouses.

The quotes inside our cookies were corny but still made us smile. Hers read, *"Take a chance on someone new."* And mine announced, *"You have a secret admirer."*

CHAPTER 25

Trying hard not to worry about Connor, I made a point of keeping busy at all times by scheduling interviews in as swift succession as possible. And if not talking with anyone in person, I kept going over my notes, putting heart and soul into the investigation. Besides doctor and dentist appointments, I even allotted time to my ongoing work in progress, the writing of true crime short stories. But I failed. The problem with my son stayed always in the back of my mind.

Parents seemed to always be the last ones to know about delinquent behavior of their kids. My ex-wife and her current husband should have had at least an inkling of Connor's trouble, had they paid attention. That type of reasoning made me think of the Hoàng family. Was it possible that Tho and Lan didn't have a clue what their son was up to, and Jim had developed an opioid habit after all? Would the sister have known or at least suspected? That train of thought would tip the scale back to the original verdict of *accidental death by overdose*.

I shook my head at my illogic. His girlfriend and/or one of his fellow students would have known. Years of experience as a detective had taught me that at least someone, and most likely more than one person, always knew. Could people have been lying to me to preserve Jim's image?

My awareness crept right back to Connor again. What would I get myself into if I decided that he should come live with me? He may turn out to be hostile, full of resentment at having to move to California against his will. And what did I really know about the type of person he had become? Connor was only seven when his mom and I split, and from then onward, I had no longer taken part in bringing him up. Not that I ever had a big say in that respect even before the divorce. His mom had put herself in charge and spoiled him rotten, from what I remembered of those days.

Apart from his occasional visits and my even fewer trips to the East Coast, I'd had no physical contact with my son in the last ten years. Short phone calls, e-mails, and infrequent skype sessions hadn't done much for father-son bonding. Long-distance relationships didn't as a rule work for couples, and they worked even less for parenting, I had determined, long before facing the current Connor crisis.

At that point in my musing I welcomed the distraction of the phone ringing. I checked caller I.D. and answered it with, "Hi, Tho. What's up?"

"Just checking how you're coming along," he said.

"I'm working on it. Be patient." And I asked, "How well do you know your next-door neighbors, whose daughter was friends with Jim? I believe you said her name is Zoe."

"Fairly well. Their last name is Roberts."

"Do you happen to have their phone number?"

"I do. But why would you want to talk with them?"

"Not with the entire family. I just want to interview Zoe."

"Hold on. I'll get it for you," he said, then did.

CHAPTER 26

Zoe Roberts, I soon learned, had a busy schedule. An interview with her had to wait several days until Friday, November 30. She was an undergraduate student at the California Institute of Technology in Pasadena and agreed to meet with me for lunch at a bakery on Lake Avenue, a ten-minute walk from Caltech. The place had spacious outdoor seating, which was ideal for our purpose. I parked the Jeep at nearby Macy's parking garage, walked over and looked around. She didn't seem to be there yet, so I stationed myself in front of the bakery's entrance.

I had mentioned what I looked like and what I would be wearing over the phone. She soon jogged over to me, and slightly out of breath said, "You must be Nick Fox, although I saw plenty of other men wearing beige trousers and baseball caps on my run over."

I paid for our orders of croissants filled with ham and cheese and two bottled waters, which we carried outside. After exchanging a few pleasantries, we ate our lunch in silence, which gave me an opportunity to study her. She was slim, wearing a tracksuit and sneakers, had her brown hair pulled into a ponytail, and as far as I could judge, wore no makeup on her rosy face.

Once we started our talk, it became clear that she was a no-nonsense young woman with above-average intelligence and a certain amount of street smarts.

I started with, "How do you like Caltech?"

She replied, "It's an excellent place of learning opportunities, and convenient for me. It takes me only 20 minutes to drive the 14 miles from Burbank."

"Was it costly to enroll?"

"I got a scholarship. There would have been no way my parents could have afforded to send me. The scholarship covers most of the tuition, but not fees, meals, books and supplies, or personal expenses. I have to work to make ends meet."

"So what do you study?"

"I'm carrying a full load and looking at a master's degree in Aerospace Engineering. After that, I'm planning to enroll in pilot training. One of the places I'm considering is Glendale Community College. They have an excellent program which includes ground classes and flight labs in preparation to pass the pilot certification approved by the FAA."

"That's the Federal Aviation Administration, correct?"

She rolled her eyes. "What else?"

"So you're planning to become a pilot?" I asked.

"For starters. In time, I hope to become an astronaut."

"I see, you're reaching for the stars."

She got my joke and said, "And beyond!"

We had long finished eating our croissants and I asked, "Can I get you dessert, coffee, or tea?"

"I'm fine. No, thanks," she said, clearly not much interested in food.

"With a full load, I'm surprised you have time to work."

She stated, "I'm a fast learner and only work part time. It's doable."

"What sort of a job do you do?"

"Up until recently, all sorts. Data entry, museum tour guide, tutoring high school kids in math and science, you name it. And now, since I turned 21, I'm an Uber driver. That really suits me. I can arrange my workhours according to my own schedule. And the money is not bad for doing nothing more than driving people from A to B."

She grinned and said, "Who knows? Next time you use Uber for a ride to the airport or somewhere, you may find me behind the wheel."

CHAPTER 27

The time had come to get to the purpose of our meeting.

Zoe began, "So you're looking into what happened to Jim Hoàng. I doubt that I can help you, but what do you want to know?"

"I've talked to a slew of people already - - mostly peers from his drama class - - about his fateful last night. In doing so, I got an idea of what kind of person he was. His dad mentioned that you and Jim were not only neighbors but good friends. So tell me first about your relationship with him."

She stated, "I'd known Jim as long as I can remember. We went to Kindergarten, elementary, and middle school together and spent a great deal of time at each other's houses. Starting ninth grade, he attended Citadel High School, and I had no choice but to continue with public schooling. We still stayed friends, though."

I asked, "What did you generally do when spending time together?"

"We played chess, backgammon, and the Japanese game of Go, and for a short time we were into Dungeons and Dragons. We also researched and built science projects, either for school or our own pleasure. Later, I sometimes helped him with his dog-walking jobs."

"It must have been hard to keep a friendship going once you went to different high schools."

"Not really. He was loyal." She smiled and reminisced, "Neither Jim or I were particularly athletic but in tenth grade we started going on short jogs together, twice a week around the neighborhood. He thought it was important to maintain an agile body and mind. We kept it up all through high school, and I'm still jogging these days, although alone."

I remarked, "I can tell that the two of you were close."

"True. But the relationship was purely platonic."

"Your mentioning loyalty reminded me that Sean Brooks said the same about Jim. Do you happen to know Sean?"

"Sure," she replied. "They were friends all through high school. Early on, Sean's mom dropped him off at Jim's house, and after getting his own driver's license, he drove over himself. Sometimes the three of us hung out together."

"Do you still keep in touch?"

"No, we lost contact after Jim died."

"What about Jim's girlfriend, Melissa Van der Molen? Did you also know her?"

Zoe's body stiffened and her former pleasant face grimaced, as if she had bitten into a lemon. She said, "I couldn't avoid knowing her."

"You resented her?"

"That's an understatement."

I stayed silent, knowing that more was to come.

She stared into the distance, watching pedestrians walking along Lake Avenue, without appearing to see them. Then she glanced back at me, opened her mouth, and her angry words broke out in rapid succession. "That bitch manipulated Jim from the first time she stepped into the Hoàngs' home to get tutored until the day he died. She bewitched him with her beauty, charming ways, and what she called "cultural tastes." Jim was putty in her hands and didn't know it. She tried - - and to a certain amount succeeded - - changing him."

Coming up for air, she continued, "Dammit! He had a logical, scientific mind. All this interest in drama plays and musical shit wasn't him."

I put in, "But I was told that he had a good voice."

"Jim could learn how to do anything he put his mind to. He taught himself how to sing by listening and singing along to that musical on iTunes or YouTube, over and over again."

She continued her rant as if I hadn't interrupted. "I attempted to make Jim realize what she was doing to him, but he stonewalled any criticism of her. As far as he was concerned, she could do no wrong. One day, when she showed up next door with her fancy car before Jim was home, I went over and gave her a piece of my mind. I told her that I knew what she was doing. With a nasty smile on her lips and hands on her hips, she looked me in the eye and remarked, 'Well, it's working, isn't it!'"

Zoe teared up and added, "She didn't just sleep with him, the bitch had to have his soul too."

She got herself back in control and said, "Sorry about the outburst. I didn't realize until just now that I still cared."

I changed the subject, asking, "What can you tell me about the Hoàng family and their relationships with Jim?"

"His parents were hardworking and kind. He had a close connection with his grandma. They seemed to have their own little jokes and understandings, leaving outsiders clueless. There was Jennifer, his younger sister, who could be a pill at times."

"How do you mean?"

"Jim was sort of in charge of her while his parents minded their store, which was not an easy task. He believed everything she told him, the trusting guy that he was. But I happen to know that she got away with murder."

She clasped her hand over her mouth and said, "Sorry, under the circumstance that was uncalled for."

I asked, "Was Jennifer into drugs or drinking?"

"Oh no, nothing like that. It was mostly boys and places she was not allowed to go to."

"How did you know?"

"She had boys sneaking in and out of their house when Jim was busy with after-school activities. The grandma was half deaf and unaware of what was going on. I mentioned it to Jim once and he questioned her. She maintained that she and the boys were studying together, and he believed her. And one Saturday afternoon, I saw her and a girlfriend coming out of a movie theater where they had watched an R-rated film, which at 15, she obviously was not permitted to see. They must have used fake IDs."

CHAPTER 28

The bakery's outdoor table and chairs covered by sun umbrellas had been emptied and then re-occupied by patrons all around us, but nobody seemed to mind that we were still there, with our food long consumed and nothing but the two almost empty water bottles in front of us.

I said, "Let's move on to Jim's tragic night. Did you by chance attend the opening night of the musical *Woeful?*"

She replied, "I hadn't planned to nor did I want to go. Seeing Jim make a fool of himself on stage was not something I'd have cared to witness."

"But?"

"Just before going to Citadel on that Saturday, he came over to my house and talked me into going with him. I had all sorts of reservations, but he wouldn't take no for an answer. When I protested that I didn't have a ticket, he said that they could be bought at the door. And when I pointed out that I'd be there two-and-a-half hours early, he said that I could stay in the school's library until the auditorium doors opened to the public. When I complained that I wouldn't be able to eat dinner, he told me not to worry, he'd figure something out.

"I guess he knew that I didn't think he had any acting talent and was out to prove me wrong. So I finally gave in and off we went. On the car ride over to Lake View Terrace, he was full of self-confidence. He seemed to be giddy in anticipation of his performance. He was alternately humming or whistling his imminent solos.

"Once we got to his school, true to his word, he dropped me off at the library and promised to find out about food. There were a few kids reading and doing research at the computer lab on that late Saturday afternoon, but nobody seemed to notice me. I found a fairly current NASA science book about the robotic spacecraft mission *New Horizons*. I was particularly interested in the confirmation of the existence of a "hydrogen wall" at the outer edges of the solar system.

"I admit that I got involved with the book and almost jumped when Jim came to fetch me for dinner. The good law-abiding citizen that he was, Jim had actually asked his drama teacher if I could eat with the theater cast. Can you imagine?"

It was a rhetorical question and she didn't expect a comment, but I thought to myself, voilà, the identity of the mystery girl who appeared out of nowhere to eat pizza with the cast and crew is solved.

She continued, "Melissa was giving me nasty looks during the entire meal. I could tell that she had no idea why I was there. For once she wasn't in control, and I had one over on her. To my surprise, Jim handed me a ticket for the show and said he was treating me. Then I went back to the library until they opened the auditorium doors."

When she hesitated I said, "I know what follows is painful for you to talk about, but I need to hear your full account."

So she went on, "To my surprise, I liked the musical. Everyone sang and acted well, and I couldn't believe what I saw and heard when Jim came on stage. He was electrifying and moving, all in one. He stumbled a bit in the last act, but I thought that it was all part of the show. And when he collapsed, I still thought that it was make-believe. It wasn't until the drama teacher asked about a doctor in the audience that I started to wonder if something had gone wrong backstage. And when he announced that everyone should leave except for the Hoàngs, and at the same time I heard sirens outside, I knew that it had to do with Jim. I wasn't about to leave, but rushed up behind the curtain, after his family."

She touched her own throat and said, "There he lay, all distorted and gasping for breath. I'll never forget it, no matter how long I live. The paramedics worked on him and then rushed him to the hospital. Jim's dad followed in his car, taking grandma and Jennifer with him. I showed his mom where the Toyota was parked and she gave me a ride in Jim's car. At the hospital we waited in the emergency area until a doctor came and told us the bad news."

Her sad eyes met mine as she added, "I'm sure you know that Jim passed away in the ambulance."

I nodded, and without another word, she got up and waved good-bye. She seemed to be overcome with grief.

CHAPTER 29

I stayed seated by the bakery a while longer, pondering the conversation I'd had with Zoe Roberts. Becoming an astronaut was an ambitious quest, but she seemed smart and goal-oriented enough to succeed.

It amazed me that such a pragmatic young woman could have shown so much fury when talking about Melissa. It was clear to me that, no matter the platonic relationship she may have had with Jim, deep down she had been in love with him, whether aware of it or not. And I could also envision that he himself had been clueless about that fact.

She was the second person who had told me that there had been a special bond between Jim and his grandmother. Too bad that my interview with the old lady had been so brief. Another chat with Mai Hoàng was indicated, I decided. Also, Zoe had touched on Jim's whistling habit, a small piece of information that others had also mentioned. It may not be important at all, but just in case, I planned to look at my notes later to check who else had remarked about it and in what context.

The piece of information I had gathered about Zoe being the mystery girl who was present at Jim's last meal gave me no choice but to add her to my list of suspects. Granted, her showing up at the auditorium had not been planned, so she would have been unprepared to do the deed. But she may have been lying, and the ride to the school with Jim had been on her agenda all along.

The slip she made about Jennifer getting away with murder was priceless, I chuckled to myself. And the idea entered my head, was it really a slip or had the clever young woman made the remark deliberately, with calculation?

It occurred to me that I had forgotten to ask her opinion whether she believed the verdict of accidental death caused by an opioid overdose was correct, or if she thought that her friend had either committed suicide or was murdered. I wondered what else I had omitted to question her about. All of a sudden I was struck by the knowledge that it was Zoe who had set off our discussion and steered it in the direction of her comfort zone.

The woman was smart and competent. Of all the people I had interviewed so far, I would tag her as being the most capable to plan and execute a perfect murder, without getting caught. She would be the type of killer that kept a cool head throughout.

The passionate tantrum she displayed when our talk turned to Melissa seemed out of character. I could have sworn, though, that the outburst was spontaneous and genuine. Or could it have been a calculated ploy?

I shook my head in frustration, got up, and walked in the direction of the Macy's garage.

CHAPTER 30

Bearing in mind that I had talked with all other witnesses in person, I opted not to make an exception with Andrew Baldoni by questioning him by phone or skype but rather to wait until he came home for Christmas break. Meanwhile, I attempted to schedule a meeting with Sergeant Anna Diego, the main investigating detective of the closed case.

The sergeant was a busy woman and not easy to get a hold of. When I finally reached her, she was less than pleased with the idea of possibly reopening a case that had been closed for three years, having plenty on her plate with current work. However, she graciously agreed to see me on her day off, at 10:00 a.m., on Thursday, December 13, fitting me in among running errands and getting a haircut.

During my years on the force, I had worked with Sergeant Diego on occasion and found her competent and also compassionate. She lived in Sunland, and we met in her neighborhood park. I got there first and walked around before settling on a picnic bench. The park was relatively empty on that weekday morning. A few homeless lay still asleep, a couple of dog owners played with their pets, a handful of parents watched their pre-school kids in the equipment area, and a match was in progress on the tennis court. I watched two teenage boys tossing and catching a Frisbee, and briefly wondered why they were not in school.

While waiting for her, I reflected that the sergeant would be in her early forties by now. At that moment she made her way over to me, and I thought that there was something different about her but couldn't pin it down.

She greeted me, then looked down in the general direction of my leg and said, "I didn't want to bother you after what happened, knowing that you wouldn't appreciate being pitied."

"You've got that right. Besides, I remember getting a nice card from you." And I remarked, "Thanks for making time for me today."

She brushed it off with a hand gesture, grabbed a cellphone from her back jeans pocket, and said, "I've familiarized myself already with the inactive case and since actual reports and documentations can't be taken out of the department, I've downloaded the Hoàng files to my phone and am willing to compare notes with you."

"Fair enough. I'm particularly interested in the interviews of witnesses."

I suddenly realized what was different about her. She used to have long, dark hair, worn in a severe bun or ponytail. It was still dark but cut short in a becoming style. I burst out, "It's your hair!"

"Pardon?"

"You've cut it."

She laughed. "I'm surprised you noticed." Then she got down to business and said, "First of all, what drew your attention to the inactive case?"

"Tho Hoàng is my friend. He asked me to do a bit of unofficial private investigating, since he believes that his son was murdered."

"I remember Mr. Hoàng clearly. He was adamant that his son was not an opioid user." She checked the info on her phone and quoted, "His exact words were 'Someone did this to Jim.' I sympathized with him at the time, and I still sympathize with him now, but parents don't always know what goes on with their teenage kids."

Then her dark eyes focused on me as she stated, "Rest assured, my colleague and I did a thorough investigation and there was no evidence whatsoever of foul play."

"I'm aware of that but may come up with new evidence," I countered.

"You know good and well that your so-called new evidence must meet certain requirements before a court would agree to vacate a judgement. You have to be in possession of that new evidence, in other words, it must exist. A suggestion that it might exist is not enough."

"Okay, I'm going to be honest with you and lay my cards on the table. I've read the coroner's autopsy report - - you don't have to show me the record - - and know exactly what Jim Hoàng died of. It's all cut and dry, and I'm not disputing any of it, nor am I implying that you didn't do an excellent job of investigating.

"At this point, though, I'm convinced that he did not accidentally overdose nor commit suicide. The only other possibility is that someone else took his life by adding a lethal dose of pain killers to his food or drink. I have formed a few ideas of who the culprit might be but so far am unable to narrow it down to one person. As soon as I know for sure, I will find the evidence, even if it means tricking someone into giving it.

"For now, let's compare notes. I suggest that we go over each testimony given to you by persons you questioned at the time and match them up with my interviews. Small discrepancies here and there would be natural as we can't expect people's memories to be perfect. We're looking for gross differences in their statements that would alter the facts."

So we did just that. Meticulously going over her witness statement records taken from her phone and comparing them to my tablet entries of interviews and my comments about each person I had talked to. Overall, we could not find any major inconsistencies, which was a disappointment to me.

Some people had volunteered more information talking with me than they did three-and-a-half years previously to the police, which was only natural. Part of it was that they tended not to be at ease when questioned by the authorities, and the other reason had to do with the wording of the inquiry. Sergeant Diego had only been interested in facts, observations, and people's whereabouts, and not their opinions. For instance, Jennifer had not let on that she thought her brother had committed suicide, and most others failed to disclose that they didn't believe the overdose was accidental. By the same token, Lan Hoàng had not offered her theory to the sergeant that the pills were intended for someone other than her son.

A Frisbee landed at my feet. I picked it up and tossed it back to one of the teenagers. Then I said, "I talked to two additional witnesses, Jim Hoàng's best friend, Sean Brooks, and his next-door neighbor kid whom he'd been friends with since Kindergarten. I'm surprised that you didn't question either one."

She asked, "Were they drama class kids who took part in the musical?"

"No."

"There's your answer. It takes two to three hours for fatal symptoms to appear after overdosing on opioids. Neither one of those two could have slipped anything into the victim's food or drink, nor could they have seen anyone else doing so, since they weren't there."

"Ah, but the neighbor kid was in fact present at the scene," I said, and read her my notes of the interview I'd had with Zoe Roberts.

She listened carefully, and then admitted, "That went through the cracks, I'm sorry to say." And she added, "That's an interesting young woman, by the way."

I also showed her my account of Sean's interview and related the phone call he later made, informing me of the inappropriate conduct between a person of authority and a student. To that she commented, "I can see that could give you things to think about."

And after a few moments of staring straight ahead of herself, obviously in deep thought, she turned to me and said, "Having become familiar with your account of the case, I can see that you've arrived at a few ideas, as you put it, but I'm also going to be honest with you and lay my own cards on the table. As we've already established, the way to reopen a case is to discover and present new evidence.

"In this instance, gathering that evidence is indeed tough. Nobody admits to knowing or having seen anything incriminating. If you try hard, you can probably come up with a motive for murder, but I don't have to tell you that proof and concrete evidence is what's needed. Just your gut feeling isn't going to do the trick. You may have to resort to putting some pressure on some of your witnesses."

I said, "What about involving a lawyer or going to the press?"

"Neither would do you any good, in my opinion. Short of a confession from the killer himself, your chances are slim for reopening the case."

To say that I was disappointed would be a gross understatement. "Crushed" would express it better.

CHAPTER 31

At home that afternoon, I pulled up the computer file with all the information I had gathered so far. The file was substantial. I skipped the official documentations of police incident report, coroner's autopsy findings, and the original witness statements given to Sergeant Diego. None of that was any help to me at that point. What I needed to do was carefully go over the many pages with information of my own documented interviews and notes and try to discover important facts that I may have missed.

Although reading the data from the wide monitor of my desktop computer was easier on the eye than from the tablet, the task was still tedious. I went through it slowly and meticulously. Once I'd arrived at the last page, I applied myself to serious thinking.

I did come across several mentions of Jim's whistling. The first was from his grandma. She had remarked that when he came back from telling his friends the good news of being accepted to UCI, he had been whistling. Melissa told me that she heard Jim whistling one day and realized that he carried a perfect tune. She also shared that he had a habit of whistling when happy or having solved a problem. And Zoe commented that he was whistling when driving them to his school before the show.

This meant that he was happy on all three occasions, and it was a no-brainer as to the reasons why. In the first instance, he had just learned of his acceptance and scholarship to UCI. In the second, he was no doubt happy to be in Melissa's company, and on the third occasion, full of eagerness to perform. So why did I dwell on this whistling thing?

There was the issue of Jim's stage fright. Mai Hoàng seemed to have been the only one aware of it; everyone else had been ignorant on that account. In fact, Melissa had strongly denied its existence. Perhaps I had misunderstood the elder lady.

Since not just one, but several people had mentioned that Jim was gullible and easy to manipulate, I had to believe that it was the truth. The piece of information obtained by Sean Brooks about the alleged misconduct between a person of authority and a student that Jim had observed, was a concern. Granted, the accusation was vague with nothing concrete for me to confront, but it merited a closer look.

Alex Topalian and his eidetic memory came to mind. Why did he think the fact that he saw Jim at the water fountain several times was important enough to mention? So the boy was thirsty, big deal! I did ask that witness to tell me what he observed, so maybe according to his special type of memory, he did just that and nothing more.

Was all this connected and I could not piece the puzzle together for now? Or did some of the information not apply to my undertaking and need to be weeded out? The more I pondered over it, the more frustrated I got.

In the evening, I fixed myself a tuna sandwich, brought it over to the computer, and continued my quest. I pored over each of my suspects, focusing on opportunity and motive, one by one. At bedtime I was no more the wiser and threw in the towel.

Nick, I told myself, give it a rest!

CHAPTER 32

On the next day, I made the decision to give the investigation a break. Distancing my mind from it for a while may help. I became aware that obsessing over it only got me aggravated and defeated my purpose. The puzzle pieces would fall into place when least expected, I told myself. From years of experience on the force I knew that the longer a case was unsolved, the less likely it would be solved. The scent would have cooled off. Jim Hoàng's case had been cold for years; a few more days or weeks made no difference.

Also, it was ten days before Christmas. Time to get in the spirit, I decided. So I did a load of laundry and then went to the local mall. My parents and sister rotated celebrating Christmas at their respective houses. Last year it had taken place at my parents' in Arizona, and now it was my sister and brother-in-law's turn in Colorado. Nobody expected me to host the event. I wouldn't have had enough room and dishes, nor the desire to entertain.

We had stopped giving presents to adults in our family a while back. My long-retired parents didn't need a thing, and the rest of us acquired both necessities and luxury items all year long. What I was looking for on that trip to the mall were gifts for my niece and nephew. I could have made the purchases online but preferred the hands-on approach.

I soon got into the holiday spirit. There was no way to avoid it, with Christmas carols ringing on amplifiers all over the shopping center, small children expectantly sitting on Santa's lap, and shoppers rushing to and fro, carrying packages. I knew that my 10-year-old nephew was into Legos and good at creating all sorts of scenes by following the complex instructions of the building sets. There were so many kits to choose from, and in the end, I settled on the Remote-Controlled Stunt Racer.

A present for my niece, who would turn 13 in a couple of months, was not that easy to decide on. I had no clue what to get a girl her age. Also, I was limited as to size, since the gift had to fit into a small suitcase. When I came upon a jewelry store, I went inside on impulse. I asked the young woman behind the counter what she could recommend for a teenager, stipulating that I was unprepared to spend more than a hundred dollars.

"Does she have pierced ears?" she inquired.

"I have no idea," I replied and grabbed my phone, sending a text to my sister in the hope that I would get a quick reply, as she worked from home.

The saleswoman said, "While you wait, feel free to look around. Maybe you can find a gift for your wife - -" she glanced at my bare ring finger and realized the gaffe she'd made - - "or your significant other." Slightly embarrassed, she helped another customer who had entered the store behind me.

I browsed the place, feeling uncomfortable and knowing good and well that I was not interested in any major purchase. To my relief, I soon heard the ping of my sister's text. Her answer came in one word: "*Yes.*"

Minutes later, I left the jewelers with a small gift box containing a pair of sterling silver filigree hoop earrings. This concluded the extent of my Christmas shopping that year. Ever since my son became a teen, I had been in the habit of either sending a check or a gift card his way. This seemed impossible in the current year, since camp rules did not allow him to receive money, nor was he free to go to a store to redeem a gift card.

For a fleeting moment I considered getting something for Diana, but rejected the idea. I did not want her to think that she would have to respond with a gift of her own. A card might be the way to go, I determined. I had stopped sending Christmas cards out years ago but now went into a stationary store to select one.

Living alone, I never bothered with a Christmas tree or other decorations, but when I stopped at the supermarket on my way home on that Friday in mid-December, I found myself in a festive mood and bought a large poinsettia plant.

The following morning I reconsidered and wrote a check to Connor. I mailed it to my ex-wife with a note attached that read, *"I doubt that Connor is permitted to receive money where he is, but I cannot bring myself to overlook him this Christmas. Do with it what you feel is best."*

CHAPTER 33

My sister and her family lived in a suburb near Denver, Colorado. Our parents had named her Catherine, but everyone except Mom - - who refuses to use shortened names - - called her Cathy. I had planned my visit from Sunday, December 23 to Wednesday the 26th and booked a roundtrip flight accordingly. Before packing my bag I went online and checked the weather in Denver for the next few days: High 45 and low 19 degrees Fahrenheit, no snow. Brrr! I didn't own a winter coat, so I dug out my old ski jacket at the back of the wardrobe closet.

The flight time was one hour and 50 minutes, but I knew from past experience that the gate-to-gate time was more like two-and-a-half hours. My brother-in-law came to fetch me at the airport. I landed at 3:30 p.m., and by the time I was out of the terminal, walked to where his car was parked, and was chauffeured to their home, it was close to six o'clock. So I basically only had two full days of visiting, Christmas Eve and Christmas Day, since I left on the morning of the 26th.

My parents were already there and came to greet and hug me as soon as I stepped through the front door. They looked well. Years of retirement agreed with them. I handed my sister the two bottles of wine I had purchased at the airport. Even though adults didn't exchange presents in my family, I thought that was the least I could contribute to the Christmas meal.

The ranch-style single family house had four bedrooms. My parents were given the guest bedroom, equipped with a queen bed. In previous years, I had slept on the sofa in the living room, and I was pleasantly surprised when my nephew offered me his bed and resolved to sleep on an air mattress on the floor.

Both kids were busy with their own activities on that first evening. My niece attended a holiday event at her school, and my nephew was invited to a friend's party. We five adults ordered Thai food and had it delivered.

Cathy was a self-employed accountant working from home. Her clientele were small businesses in need of professional help with their bookkeeping. But the bulk of her income came from preparing people's tax return forms, which got hectic from January until April during tax season. My brother-in-law was a surgical nurse with 8- to 10-hour shifts.

Mom addressed him, "So you're off for the next three days?"

"Sure am, unless I get called in for emergency surgery," he replied.

The conversation turned to the Utah camping trip my sister and her family had taken in the fall. My brother-in-law elaborated on the fantastic hoodoos they had admired when visiting Bryce Canyon, describing these rock formations in great detail. Then he told about the adventure they had experienced trekking the Narrows at Zion National Park. The family had hiked waist-deep in the river, which ran canyon wall to canyon wall.

Mom gave her account of our parents' recent stay at Maui, Hawaii. Going out on a deep-sea fishing boat in particular had captivated her. She remarked, "We had lots of romance too. Sort of like a second honeymoon. Didn't we?" she said, glancing at Dad.

Visibly embarrassed he murmured, "If you say so."

She then inquired into her granddaughter's activities, like dance and flute lessons and the ensuing recitals of each. Dad wanted to know all about the accomplishments of his grandson's soccer team. When that discussion was exhausted, Mom turned to me.

She said, "And what's new with you, Nicklaus?"

I had no intention of telling them about what was currently going on with Connor. Both Mom and Dad would have wanted details I was unable to provide. And I certainly did not want to mention Diana. Knowing Mom, she would have jumped to conclusions, asking all sorts of embarrassing questions. I also hesitated to bring up the Hoàng business, as I tried not to dwell on it for the time being.

So I said, "I started on a project of writing a book about true crime short stories."

Mom stated, "Well, that may keep you busy but doesn't get you in contact with the outside world. Don't become a recluse. You need to get out and meet people."

I laughed and said, "Doubtless you mean meet women. You never give up, do you?"

"That's partly what I meant, but seriously, you need to interact with other human beings. Don't hide yourself away."

"As a matter of fact, I've had plenty of human contact lately," I countered, and reluctantly told them about the sleuthing job I was doing for my friend Tho. Even though I had initially tried to avoid the subject, I now warmed up to it. After all, Dad was an ex-cop too with lots of experience under his belt. Maybe he could give me advice. I told them what the case was about and gave a short version of my interviews with the suspects.

In conclusion I stated, "I can't picture any of them as a cold-blooded killer."

Mom remarked that she'd read that under certain circumstances anyone was capable of murder. She also stated that emotions ran wild with teenagers and that more often than not their actions were irrational and irresponsible. It was all due to hormones, she declared. And then she went into a spiel of how my sister had been out of control at times during her teens.

Cathy protested, "Get real, Mom. Sure, I was a handful, but you can hardly compare my unruly behavior in those days to that of a killer!"

"Of course not. I'm just saying that kids that age are unpredictable because emotions dictate their actions. They sometimes cannot control their urges."

Then she turned to me and said, "I was hoping that the dangerous cop business was in the past for you but it looks like you can't stay away from it."

"Don't worry, Mom. I'm not in any danger."

Dad, a man of few words, had been silently enjoying his food and was ready to speak now. "All your suspects who hung out near the victim during his last meal had opportunity to drop a fatal dose of pills into his drink unobserved. On the other hand, I doubt that it could have been added to the pizza as easily, without anyone noticing. I recommend that you concentrate on motive."

He reached over and tapped me on the shoulder, saying, "You'll get there in the end, I'm sure of it."

Much later in the evening, when Dad and I had a private moment together, he said, "Son, I did not want to say this in front of your mother, but I'm sure you know that there is always a chance of personal danger involved whenever someone looks into a cold case."

I couldn't argue with that.

CHAPTER 34

We kept the family tradition alive by celebrating on Christmas Eve and again on Christmas Day. On the 24th we would have a festive meal, followed by singing Christmas carols accompanied by my niece's flute. Without fail, Mom would admire the ornaments on the floor-to-ceiling tree, commenting on every single one. Then at long last, the kids would open their gifts. The next morning, Santa would leave a most-wished-for present for each of them and fill their stockings.

The current year was no exception. The prime rib was done to perfection and the dinner conversation was lighthearted. My offerings were a hit with the kids; my niece especially seemed thrilled with the earrings.

She cried out, "Uncle Nick! How did you know I only wear silver or white gold, never any yellow or rose gold?"

"A lucky guess," I grinned. If the truth were told, I'd have to confess that I didn't want to spend the money for any kind of gold.

Before coffee and dessert was served, I stayed in the kitchen with Cathy and helped with the dishes. The wine glasses had to be done by hand. She washed and I dried.

She said, "I'm glad I have you to myself for a few minutes. So tell me what's wrong."

"Nothing. What makes you think there is?"

"You're trying hard to be cheerful but something's bothering you. It can't just be that cold case you're investigating. I remember when you were on the force, no matter what hard and gruesome cases you'd be working on, you managed to keep them out of your private life. So what's going on?"

Cathy had always been able to read me and it came as no surprise that she still did. Grudgingly I told her about Connor.

She listened to the little I knew and then said, "Don't judge your ex-wife too harshly. A kid making a detour in the wrong direction can happen in the best of families."

"I'm aware of that. I don't really blame her. It's just that I haven't been around my son for any length of time in ten years and now, out of the blue, I've been asked to take part in parenting him come spring or summer. I don't even know whether I'm fit to handle a troubled teen."

"Part of the 'repair' might be taken care of while he's at that camp. It actually makes sense that he should not go back to the same environment and friends when he gets out. If you decide to have him live with you for a year or so, you have my total support."

"Thanks!"

We were done washing dishes, and as we carried dessert and coffee cups into the dining room I thought, this is the second time I'm offered support with my dilemma. First my ex-partner Rick attested to it and now my sister. Generous of them, I suppose, but what real help would they be? Connor would be living under my roof, not theirs.

My brother-in-law was Catholic, and most years he, and whoever was still awake enough by that hour, attended midnight mass. The church was a ten-minute drive away, and by 11:30 p.m. both kids were ready for bed and so was Dad. In previous years I also skipped the event, but now I felt that a bit of praying couldn't hurt with my problem. We bundled up and were ready to brave the below-freezing temperature outside. I even borrowed a ski hat. Mom looked like a mummy, wearing several layers of clothing under her coat and a heavy scarf over her head.

Cathy remarked, "Mom, we get into the car inside the garage and the walk from the church parking lot is about 50 yards!"

"I have thin Arizona blood," our mother shot back.

I didn't understand what was going on at the altar during mass, and there was lots of standing up, kneeling, sitting, and standing up again, but the priest gave a solid sermon, and listening to the choir was a delight.

I had barely fallen asleep the next morning, it seemed, when I heard my nephew scrambling out of his sleeping bag and getting up from the air mattress. Must be time to check what Santa brought, I thought, as he hurried out of the room. The kids didn't believe in Santa Claus any longer, but he still left the main present and filled the stockings. I promptly dozed off again.

When I showed up in the living room hours later, I found my brother-in-law huddled on the floor over a pair of skis, adjusting the bindings to boots.

"Looks like Santa left new equipment," I remarked.

My nephew grinned from ear to ear and said, "He must have known that I outgrew my skis and boots."

My niece modeled a brand-new ski outfit and I said, "Bet you can't wait hitting the slopes."

"We're going to Echo Mountain the day after tomorrow!"

The kids spent a good part of the day playing with their new toys and building the Lego Remote-Controlled Stunt Racer. In the late afternoon, we all watched the movie *It's a Wonderful Life*. For dinner we ate the leftovers from Christmas Eve.

I had just stuffed a piece of meat into my mouth, when Mom asked, "Are you seeing Connor between Christmas and New Year's?"

Taking my time answering, I chewed, swallowed, and then said, "He's busy elsewhere this year."

My sister, realizing that I did not want to discuss Connor with Mom or anyone else at the dinner table, came to the rescue and changed the subject, asking Mom about some recipe for carrot cake. I sent a thankful glance in her direction.

On the flight home the next morning I thought, like always, I enjoyed getting together with my folks, and like always, I was happy to get away again.

CHAPTER 35

Andrew Baldoni was anything but enthusiastic about setting aside time to see me on his holiday break. I couldn't blame him. He had planned to engage in fun activities during his home visit, and getting questioned about the Jim Hoàng issue wasn't one of them.

When we first talked on the phone he said, "Why stir this up again? Leave Jim in peace in his grave."

I countered, "I don't know about Jim, but his parents are unable to get peace until the matter is resolved. You wouldn't want that on your conscience."

He caved in under that kind of pressure and agreed to meet at his parents' house in Woodland Hills on Friday afternoon, December 28.

I found the place in an upscale neighborhood and parked on the circular driveway. The home was near mansion size but I only got to see one room of its interior. The entrance hall had a couple of upholstered chairs, and that was as far as Andrew let me advance. I guessed that his parents were either at work or elsewhere, and that there was no servant or housekeeper present. At least no sound could be heard beyond the foyer. The house was dead still.

He motioned me into one of the chairs and then sat down in the other. They were comfortable, I admitted to myself. Glancing at my host, I saw a young man that I labeled in my mind as "Italian looking." He had a full head of short dark hair, and there was a determined expression in his brown eyes.

I said, "I've interviewed everyone else concerned, meaning former students and staff of Citadel High School, who came in contact with Jim Hoàng on the day he died. You are the last person on my list. According to my records, the character Aurelius you portrayed in the musical was Peterus's rival, played by Jim."

He nodded.

And I came straight to the point, saying, "I understand that you were not only his rival on the stage. There was also rivalry between you and Jim in real life."

He protested, "That was real malicious of Melissa to bring up. It didn't mean a thing and happened over a year earlier."

"Tell me in your own words, please."

"Okay, she may have already told you that she and I were an item. Then, when she got tutored by Jim toward the end of our junior year, she dropped me and went out with him. Melissa was my first love - - at least I thought so at the time. I was humiliated but also furious at Jim and threatened him."

"Threatened him how?" I asked.

"Oh, it was silly kid stuff. Teenagers can get overly emotional, I'm sure you agree."

"True, but I'd still like to know the threat."

"I told him that he'd better stay away from Melissa or he and everyone concerned wouldn't live to regret it." He added, "As I said, I didn't really mean it. The outburst was spontaneous and came as a result of being deeply upset that the girl had broken up with me."

He grinned and added, "Thinking back to it now, it was nothing but a melodramatic teenage reaction and spiteful of Melissa to mention."

I grinned back at him and stated, "Melissa didn't bring up the subject. Your account is the first I've heard of it. What I was referring to about a rivalry between you and Jim I learned from Ms. Deschamps, the high school principal. She commented that there was an academic competition going on between the two of you."

He bit his lip, and I could tell that he hated himself for having let the cat out of the bag. He recovered fast, though, and remarked, "Correct. I was in the math and computer science club, where he beat me to the presidency. Monthly competitions were held in that club. We also occasionally were on opposite sides of debate teams."

"Interesting," I said. "I've heard of high school debate teams but never learned what it involved. Tell me a bit about the process."

"It's rather simple. A debate is an argument with rules. Two teams are given a topic, and each team has an allotted time to prepare an argument. Debate subjects are not revealed in advance, so the idea is to come up with a convincing argument in a short amount of time. It helps if students are familiar with current events and controversial issues.

"They take positions of either pro or con. Then the teams discuss the topic and deliver statements. The opposition's arguments are then discussed and the teams have to come up with rebuttals. Then they make their closing statements. A judge or sometimes several judges assign points based on the strength of the arguments of the teams, and then declare the winner."

I commented, "You explained that well, thanks. I take it that the debates can get heated?"

"Sure. Especially when students feel strongly about a subject."

"Like you and Jim felt when on opposite teams?"

He gave an embarrassed snicker and admitted, "We both got intense at times but that was part of the fun."

"Besides being rivals in more than one way, what can you tell me about Jim Hoàng?"

"He was smart, no doubt about that. He could do the math of any given science or other problem better and faster than anyone else. He was also knowledgeable in most subjects. It was amusing to me that, even given his intelligence, he didn't understand sarcasm."

"Are you saying that he took sarcasm literally?" I asked.

"Exactly. Some people had fun with that, including me, I have to admit."

"Now then," I said, "let's get to the opening night of the musical *Woeful,* performed by your high school drama class. Did you notice anything odd or different about Jim or anyone else in the cast, either before or during the performance?"

He took a moment to think about it and then stated, "Not that I can recall. We were all excited before show-time, which was normal, and the performance itself went without a hitch."

"The way the musical was explained to me is that you and Jim were together on stage in the last act, just before he collapsed."

"That's right. I joined him on stage the moment he finished singing his solo. I said my last line, pulled out my dagger and performed a make-believe stabbing. Then I turned the dagger on myself in a staged suicide. We lay next to each other pretending to be dead. As soon as the curtain had come down, I got up and didn't realize until later that Jim hadn't done likewise, following me off the stage."

"You didn't notice anything different about him during that last performance before he fell down?"

"At the time I didn't. Later, when I knew what happened, I thought that he staggered more than he had done previously during rehearsals. I may have imagined this, however."

I was trying to think of more questions to ask him when the connecting door to the garage flew open and an energetic woman, carrying several packages, passed us by with big strides, crying out, "I swear the mall is more crowded now than it was before Christmas!"

Then she noticed me, stopped in her tracks, and said to Andrew, "Oh, you have company."

Andrew made the introduction, "Meet my mom." And to her, "I told you about my appointment with the investigator. This is him, Mr. Fox."

She turned to me and said, "Oh yes, you're looking into the matter of that Vietnamese boy that died so tragically at Citadel when Andrew attended." And to her son, "Why didn't you ask him inside the house?"

I intervened, "This spot is fine and we're just about done."

She remarked, "Citadel is an excellent high school and was well worth the money and the 35-minute ride out of my way until Andrew was old enough to drive himself. I am convinced it is thanks to the education he got there that he was accepted to the elite university he's attending now."

She shook a finger at me and stated, "You cannot possibly blame the school for what happened to that poor boy."

Before I had a chance to comment she continued, "Well, I'll leave you two to it," and took herself and her packages to the interior of the house.

My final question to the young man was, "What's your major?"

"I'm studying law," he replied, "following in the footsteps of my dad."

CHAPTER 36

Traffic was heavy on the US-101 South. The 20-mile drive home took 40 minutes, which I spent mulling over the meeting with Andrew Baldoni. An interesting interview in many ways, I determined.

I knew that the young man was beating himself up this very moment about having jumped to the conclusion that I was talking about a rivalry between him and Jim over Melissa. Assuming that Melissa had already told me about the threat he made, caused him to come clean about it. The expression on his face was priceless as I mentioned that his admission was news to me. As for the threat itself, it could have been a harmless teenage outburst, like he implied, or it may have run deeper.

By the same token, the academic rivalry could have been all fun and games, as he suggested, or not. The fact that Jim took sarcasm literally and that Andrew and others had at times had "fun with that" was a bit of interesting news. His account of opening night of the musical was straightforward and tallied with what I had learned from other witnesses. The mention that Jim's staggering seemed more pronounced than at rehearsals, and that Andrew may have imagined this later, made sense either way.

I judged the young man to have above-average intelligence and could well imagine a battle of minds between him and Jim.

What's more, he liked the sound of his own voice, which was evident when he explained the mechanics of high school debate teams. He was good at rhetoric, I noticed. That he studied law came as no big revelation. I could picture him as a trial attorney, strutting back and forth before a jury, making clever arguments.

Andrew's mother was a firecracker and it occurred to me that I wouldn't want to earn her wrath. It was remarkable that she thought I was investigating the matter for a possible lawsuit against the school. That people would get that idea had never entered my mind. But coming from someone whose husband was a lawyer - - and whose son was aiming to become one - - I was not surprised in the least.

CHAPTER 37

Saturday, December 29, was a day when I received phone calls galore from concerned people. The first was from Tho, who seemed apologetic. After inquiring how the investigation was coming along and my reply that I was getting a handle on it, he got to the purpose of his call. The conversation went something like this:

He said, "I know that you're keeping on top of things, and I don't want to be a pest, but my mother came up with a suspect whom you may not be aware of. You asked us all if Jim had any enemies, and we couldn't think of any. 'Enemy' might be too strong a word, but Mother remembered a boy with whom Jim was in intense competition throughout his high school years."

He didn't give me a chance to interrupt and went on, "We kept the program of the musical, which showed pictures of the cast members. It turns out that the boy my mother was referring to was also one of the performers of *Woeful*."

I stated, "That would be Andrew Baldoni, whom I interviewed yesterday."

"Oh! Sorry for meddling," he said, and we hung up.

Next I received a call from Melissa who said, "I just thought of something I forgot to tell you. Zoe, who was Jim's neighbor, had dinner with us in the auditorium on opening night."

"Thanks for the heads-up, but someone else already informed me about it. When I talked with the young woman, she confirmed the fact. By the way, did you know her prior to the night in question?"

"Sure. She hung around Jim's house a lot. If you ask me, she was in love with him and consequently hated me."

I was about to fix myself a sandwich for lunch when the phone rang again. This time it was Sean.

He started with, "I hope you're making progress with your sleuthing." Not expecting an answer, he continued, "About that inappropriate conduct Jim told me he'd witnessed between a student and someone. The more I think of it, the more I'm convinced that he meant a teacher, not just any person of authority."

"Thanks for the feedback," I said.

I was on my second attempt to seeing to lunch when I received yet another call. I wondered who else wanted to part with information I already knew.

To my delight, I heard Diana's voice, and she asked, "Do you have plans for New Year's Eve?"

"I intend to watch TV and tune in to Time Square at midnight, like most other years. You're more than welcome to join me."

"I have a better idea. How about ringing in the New Year on the Queen Mary?"

"That would be fantastic, but we're a little late. I'm sure that sold out weeks ago."

She announced, "I have tickets!"

"You're kidding?"

"I'm dead serious. A couple I'm friends with were looking forward to the bash on the ship but are both sick with the flu.

They called today and said they'd let me have their tickets if I and a guest would like to go. So, are you game?"

"Yes! Definitely, yes!"

And after a moment of consideration I said, "I assume that there'll be lots of dancing on board. I'm afraid I won't be able to take to the dance floor."

"Don't worry about that. It *is* a gala event though, so I hope you don't mind dressing up."

"Guess I'll need to rent a tuxedo?"

"That'll be perfect," she replied.

After we ended the call, I would have jumped for joy, had I still been in possession of both my legs.

Rick phoned later in the day and asked, "Want to hang out with us to celebrate New Year's?"

"Thanks for the invitation," I replied, "but I'll pass, since I have a better offer on the table," and I related my good news.

At night, I got yet another call and it was from my ex.

She said, "Thanks for Connor's check. You are correct, he is forbidden to have money at camp, but I'll save it for him."

I asked, "Was he permitted to come home for Christmas?"

"No, and we were not even allowed to go see him at camp. They consented to let me briefly talk to him on the phone. This tough love thing is as hard on me as it is on him."

Realizing that she was crying or maybe close to it, I didn't know how to respond. I ended up saying, "Hang in there," and we ended the call.

CHAPTER 38

From the moment we stepped aboard the iconic Queen Mary at 8:00 p.m. on New Year's Eve until we got off the ship at 1:00 a.m. on New Year's Day, it was a night to remember.

Diana posed a stunning picture in a moss-green, fitted, floor-length gown which highlighted her auburn hair and green eyes. My rental tux was a good fit, so I felt confident that I looked dapper for the occasion.

We roamed from room to room, each designed to represent a port the Queen Mary had sailed to in the past. All of the venues featured shows throughout the evening, and there was dancing everywhere. There was Italy, where people enjoyed fine dining and being serenaded by singers moving from table to table.

France took you into the cabaret scene at the Moulin Rouge, can-can dancers and all. We stayed there for a long time, enjoying the show while drinking Champagne. There was gambling too - - although with fake money - - and I taught Diana how to play blackjack. Once she caught on, there was no stopping her. My date was on a winning streak. The dealer turned out to be a character, keeping us in stitches with his jokes. We had so much fun, it did not matter that the money we played with wasn't real.

In the room representing Spain, we watched flamenco dancers proudly showing off their talent. The Spanish theme was one of the most popular attractions and drew a crowd, especially on the dance floor.

We spent some time in make-believe Egypt among pyramids, snake charmers, and belly dancers. After their performance, one of the dancers invited random ladies from the audience onto the stage for a brief lesson of belly dancing. Diana was one of the chosen ones, and promptly took off her shoes before doing so. Joining me after the session, she giggled and remarked, "I had no idea that belly dancing is a form of art!"

Greece was on the top deck, clearly a party area, with Greek food and non-stop dancing. Diana even talked me into taking her onto the LED dance floor and swaying to a couple of slow numbers.

Bending close to my ear to be heard above the music, she stated, "You are full of surprises, Nick. You've actually got rhythm!" Soon though, we went below again as it got too cold for her, even with wrapping a shawl over her bare shoulders.

In the Morocco venue, there was continual ethnic music and authentic food. We tasted and enjoyed the cuisine, although we had no idea what we were eating.

At around 11:40 p.m., we made our way to the bow of the ship, showcasing the New York skyline and the Statue of Liberty. We found an empty spot in the fireworks viewing area. Right as the clock struck twelve, they began.

"Happy New Year!" Diana yelled above the noise.

"Happy New Year to you too!" I shouted, pulling her close and kissing her full on the mouth.

She opened her lips and kissed me right back.

For the next 20 minutes, we sat on deck of the historic vessel and watched the fireworks above us and over the Long Beach harbor, hearing and feeling every explosion.

As the extraordinary night came to an end, and we walked hand in hand off the ship toward the parking lot, Diana said, "It *will* be a happy year. I feel it in my bones."

"I can't argue with that," I replied.

CHAPTER 39

Paying Mai Hoàng another visit was indicated. I felt certain that she could shed light on a couple of points that were unclear in my mind. I chose Friday afternoon, January 4, in the hope of finding her alone. Tho and Lan would be away tending to their store, and I counted on Jennifer being back at college after the holiday break.

There was no response when I rang the doorbell at the Hoàng residence. Remembering that the old lady was hard of hearing, I rang again and even banged my fist against the door, without result. I walked along the side of the house and heard classical music sounding out of a partially open window. I peeked inside. Sure enough, I saw her rocking to and fro in her rocking chair, humming along, while zealously crocheting away on a work in progress.

I did not want to frighten her and was undecided whether to tap against the window or call her name, when she suddenly looked straight at me.

She did not seem startled at all and, recognizing me, shouted, "Back door open. You come."

I let myself in through the patio sliding glass door and found my way to her room. She motioned me into the chair that stood against the wall, turned off the music but kept on rocking and crocheting.

"Hello, Mrs. Hoàng. What are you making?" I asked.

"Scarf," she replied.

I watched for an instant as she interlocked loops of yarn with her crochet hook in rapid succession. Although her fingers remained in a steady flow of movement, she kept her eyes on me with not so much as a glance to her handiwork.

She said, "You come back?"

"Yes," I admitted. "I hope you don't mind answering a couple more questions to get something clear in my mind."

She gave me a puzzled stare, a reminder that she was hard of hearing.

I hollered, "I have more questions. On the day of his death, Jim told you he no longer suffered from stage fright. When exactly was that?"

"When he back from friends' house."

"And I remember that you told me he was whistling when he came back."

"Yes, he whistle."

"Do you know which friends he went to see?"

She stated, "He see girlfriend and Sean."

"Anyone else?"

She shook her head.

"About the stage fright. Did he have any at rehearsals?"

"No," she replied, giving me a look that I could not interpret.

"Why not?"

This time there was no mistake about the look she shot my way. No doubt it suggested that she thought me an idiot.

She said, "No people looking."

It took me a second to get her meaning. Then I slapped my forehead and yelled, "Of course! He wasn't facing an audience during rehearsals."

I glanced out the window and, pointing to the house next door, asked, "Is that Zoe's parents place?"

She nodded and said, "Zoe home now."

At that instant, someone was backing a car down the neighbors' driveway, and I glimpsed a person with a mane of brown hair in the driver seat.

I was about to thank her for answering my questions and leave, when she pointed a finger at me and asked, "You find killer?"

"I'm getting close."

"Me help?"

"Yes, I think you did."

She gave me a knowing smile. Then she stopped her crocheting, folded the unfinished scarf, placing it in a basket at the ready next to her, and got up from the rocker.

"We drink *tra nong*," she said.

"What's that?"

"Hot tea," she translated. Although I was not a tea fan, I followed her into the kitchen, knowing that any protest would have been useless.

I watched as she boiled the water, let it stand for a minute or two, and then poured it gently into the teapot, covering it tightly and letting it brew for five minutes. While we waited, she remarked that she was treating me to lotus tea, which was a mixture of green tea and lotus flowers. At least that was the gist of what she meant, I gathered. She reached into the cupboard and took out two white porcelain oriental tea cups and sat them on the table.

When the brew was done, she poured it gracefully from the teapot into the small cups. And as we slowly sipped it, I had to admit to its fine aroma and was astonished that I didn't mind the taste in the least.

My hostess asked, "How many children you have?"

"Just one, a son."

"He good boy?"

That took me by surprise, and I had a hard time controlling my emotion as I replied, "Not right now."

She reached over and, taking my hand in both of hers, predicted, "He good boy again soon."

I don't know whether it was the soothing tea or the caring words Tho's mother had expressed about Connor, but when I let myself out the back door again, I experienced a warm and confident feeling.

CHAPTER 40

My bliss did not last long, however. As I walked along the side of the Hoàng residence, I could have sworn that a pair of eyes behind the blinds of the neighbors' window followed me with every step I took. When I reached my Jeep, parked at the curb between the two houses, I thought, get a grip old guy, nobody is stalking you. You're imagining things.

At home, I applied myself to some serious reasoning. When telling old Mrs. Hoàng that afternoon I was close to catching the killer, I hadn't been completely honest. Yes, I had an idea - - in fact I had lots of ideas - - but I was nowhere near solving the mystery.

My dad's words at Christmas when we talked about the cold case flashed back into my mind. He had pointed out that since all suspects seemed to have had opportunity to add opioids to the victim's drink unobserved, I should concentrate on motive.

And Mom's remark that emotions tended to run wild with teenagers, and that their actions were irrational and unpredictable, also popped into my head. I remembered her saying something to the effect that kids that age could not control their urges. Hell, except for the drama teacher, all my suspects were teens!

So I dwelled on motive and could in fact come up with one for most of the people who hung out with Jim during his last meal. The solution to my problem had to do with Jim himself and what kind of kid he was, I was certain of that. The fact that he was gullible, believing every word anyone told him, as well as loyal, played a major role.

I also reflected on Lan Hoàng's statement that she believed the drugs were meant for someone else and her son swallowed them by accident. If that were the case, I came up with a solid idea of the killer's actual target.

And even though I had ruled out suicide weeks ago, the words of Jennifer, Jim's sister, who had stated, "You can't force someone to swallow pills, so murder is out," would not give me any peace.

According to Sean, there was this alleged inappropriate business that Jim had witnessed between a student and - - let's assume - - a teacher. Did it even make sense that he would have needed to be silenced because of that knowledge?

A lot of the motives I came up with had to do with envy or jealousy. Could teenage spite or urges, like Mom had put it, be strong enough to result in murder? Under certain circumstances, the answer could well be yes.

There was the possibility that it was nothing but a senseless hate crime, or a sick kid who got his or her jollies by getting away with a clever random killing. On second thought, I did not believe that for even a minute.

I ended up going through all my documentation of each interview I had recorded and the many comments about witnesses and suspects I had jotted down, one last time. Frustrated, I finally gave up at 10:00 p.m. and watched the evening news instead.

CHAPTER 41

In the next few days I was busy with life in general. I had an eye doctor appointment, got a haircut, went grocery shopping, and ran other household errands. No matter how hard I tried not to dwell on it, the amateur investigation Tho had entrusted me with was a constant nag at the back of my mind.

It was early on Wednesday morning, while I played a round of golf all by myself, that I suddenly had a brainstorm. I was concentrating on putting at hole eight, when a piece of crucial information suddenly came to mind. It was something that I had neglected to document but remembered now. That bit of data made all the difference, and from that moment onward, all the puzzle pieces fell into place.

I looked at my theory from every angle, and at last the crime made sense. In fact, it stopped being theoretical and became reality. Given the circumstances, it was rather simple but effective. Against my will, I had to give the culprit credit for his ingenuity.

So I knew the why, how, where, and when, but I had no way of proving any of it. I had figured it all out but was not in possession of a shred of evidence. And after more than three years, the scent was cold, and there was almost no way to obtain that needed evidence. *Almost* was the key! If I handled it right, I could deliver the missing proof.

For a brief moment I considered whether I should start carrying my gun from here on out. Upon my honorable retirement as a police officer, I was issued an identification card with a CCW-approved endorsement, CCW being the abbreviation for "carrying a concealed weapon." I chose to leave that up to the demand of future situations.

I spent hours contemplating feasible plans of action and rejected most. Sergeant Diego's parting words at our meeting in the park came to mind: "Short of a confession from the killer himself, your chances are slim for reopening the case."

That was a tall order for sure, but having no better solution, I decided to aim in that direction. But first, I needed to get a few questions answered. Another trip to Irvine was indicated.

CHAPTER 42

It was crucial that there would be no chance of the culprit being forewarned. I remembered that Sean played golf on Thursday mornings; therefore, my idea was to show up at the Oak Creek Golf Club unannounced. Assuming that he and his friend would keep their usual tee time of 8:30 a.m., I planned to get there earlier in the hope that he would answer my questions before starting their game.

I rode out at the crack of dawn, but halfway into Orange County it started raining. By the time I reached the town of Irvine, a heavy downpour pelted my windshield, accompanied by gusty winds, making my Jeep swerve. No way would Sean and his friend venture onto the golf course in that kind of a storm. I found a safe spot to pull over to the side of the road and dialed his number.

He answered in a sleepy voice, "Yeah?"

"This is Nick Fox. Sorry! Did I wake you?" I asked.

"Yeah, when I heard the rain, I went back to sleep." And he seemed to get fully conscious and inquired, "Did you crack Jim's case?"

"Just about," I replied, "but there are a couple loose ends. Since you were his best friend, I think you might be the person to assist me at this point."

"Sure, ask away."

"I'd like to do it in person since I'm actually in Irvine at the moment."

"Come on over, then. I think my roommate has left." And he added, "I hope you're not picky; the apartment is kind of a mess."

I assured him that I did not mind an untidy place, and he gave me directions on how to get there.

Fifteen minutes later, I rang his doorbell. There had obviously not been time for him to take a shower, but it looked like he had dressed in a hurry and maybe brushed his teeth. The curly, dark hair spiraled unruly in all directions. I left my dripping umbrella by the door and followed him through the small kitchen, with dirty dishes stacked up high in the sink, to the living room. His warning over the phone of his apartment being "kind of a mess" was a gross understatement.

There were books, paperwork, dirty laundry, and what looked like maybe clean laundry strewn all over the floor, sofa, and chairs. Clutter occupied every piece of furniture and space in the room. The only objects somewhat free of litter were a desk against a wall and an office chair pulled up against it. A laptop sat on the desk, and next to it, a cup with what looked like coffee, halfway consumed.

He shoved aside some folded pieces of laundry on the sofa and beckoned me to sit down.

He asked, "Want some coffee?"

"No, thanks."

"Hope you don't mind if I finish mine," he remarked, carrying his cup with one hand and rolling the desk chair over to face me.

Then he looked me in the eye full of expectation and said, "I have no classes this morning and got plenty of time. Tell me what you've figured out."

I said, "First off, I have some questions about Jim's friend Zoe. I understand that she hung out with you and Jim. What did you think of her?"

"She was - - I mean, I'm sure she still is - - a brain." And he looked skeptical as he continued, "Don't tell me she's the villain. I simply don't believe that. She adored Jim."

"She might have targeted someone else and things went wrong."

He stared at me for a second and then cried out, "Are you suggesting that the opioid overdose was meant for Melissa?"

"That was one of my ideas, but I had plenty of others," I replied. "For instance, several people told me that Jim whistled when he was happy, but Melissa remarked that he also had a habit of whistling after successfully solving a problem. I'm sure you were aware of that."

"Yeah, he whistled a lot."

"And now to my next question. What kind of painkiller did your dad use when he hurt his back?"

"What?"

"You heard me. I propose that it was Vicodin! And don't attempt to deny it, as the fact can easily be checked."

He stared, then recovered and said, "Okay, so he took Vicodin for his pain. What has that got to do with what happened to Jim?"

"The game is up, Sean! You and I both know how it was done."

He protested, "I wasn't even there, how can you think it was me?"

"You didn't need to be near him during the crucial time at all. As I said, we both know this, but I will tell you how I've arrived at the truth. For the longest time I only tagged the people who were present at Jim's last meal as being suspects, since I assumed that someone slipped the Vicodin pills into his drink or food. That changed when I connected the dots in the last few days.

"Several witnesses mentioned that Jim was gullible and trusting, to the point of believing anything that he was told, and that he was also loyal. Yesterday, as I was playing a round of golf, I suddenly remembered what you had let slip about your dad when we were playing golf that day at the Oak Creek Golf Club. I had failed to add that crucial piece of information to my documentation, since I did not learn it during our actual interview.

"Also yesterday, it dawned on me that when Jim arrived home after his visits to Melissa and to you in the late afternoon of his fateful day, and his grandmother heard him whistling, that particular whistle was not about being happy, but rather about having solved a problem."

Sean said, "I don't understand any of this!"

"I think you do but bear with me. I figured out exactly how it was done and the motive, no doubt, was envy. First and foremost, you wanted his girlfriend, and you were also jealous about him being accepted to UCI. Now it looks like you did not get the girl after all, but you did finally make it to the university. You thought that you got away with your scheme and must have been shaken when I showed up three years later, investigating the matter."

I continued, "You were clever, making up that stuff about a student and teacher on the spur of the moment and had me fooled for a while. I was imagining all sorts of forbidden relationships between a faculty member and kid."

"What do you mean?"

"Come now, Jim never witnessed any kind of inappropriate behavior. You concocted that to throw me off the scent. And the most genius stroke on your part was admitting that you gave Jim a beer to drink on that afternoon. You probably realized that

I may figure out where he got the alcohol found in his system anyway, so confessing to it made me ignore what else could have happened at your house at that time. And now I'll tell you the details of your crime, which - -"

He interrupted, "Go ahead, I'm going to humor you and your fiction."

I went on, "Since you were his best friend, he confided in you about his stage fright. He kept it a secret from Melissa and all others of his theater crowd. The only person besides you who knew about it was his grandma. So on that Saturday afternoon, he came by to tell you about his acceptance to UCI, and knowing what kind of kid Jim was, I believe that he felt bad that you yourself had negative news from that university. Even though he did not drink alcohol as a rule, out of loyalty to you he accepted the beer.

"He either told you at that moment - - or maybe you already knew it - - of having major stage fright and his worries about the premiere that night. Knowing that he was easily manipulated and being the trusting friend that he was, you gave him the Vicodin, telling him that it would get rid of his stage butterflies. You gave him instructions of when and how many pills to take."

I added, "And for your information, Jim was seen at the water fountain several times, before show time and during intermission. I don't have to explain to you that this means he was swallowing the pills with a sip of water each time."

Without any warning, Sean broke down, yelling, "Stop already!" Tears running down his face.

CHAPTER 43

At long last he stopped sobbing and said, "That's not how it happened at all. I never meant for him to die." And he went into a spiel of his own.

"It's true, I did want Melissa. From the moment I first noticed her at Citadel in our freshman year, I was obsessed with her. I didn't stand a chance, though. She was the most popular girl in school, always surrounded by the social crowd. She had a string of boyfriends in her first three years, all among the popular people, and an entourage of girlfriends. Needless to say, neither Jim nor I were among that group.

"When Jim tutored Melissa and they soon hooked up, I was jealous. You've got that right. I assumed that their relationship would be short-lived, guessing that Melissa would get a kick out of dating a "good guy."

"What do you mean by that?" I interrupted.

"Jim was a virgin and I suspected that Melissa taught him a thing or two," he replied. "Anyhow, turns out that I was wrong. They stayed together the entire senior year."

He looked out the window, watching the rain coming down in streams. Then he focused back on me and went on, "On that Saturday, when I got the rejection from UCI, I felt sorry for myself.

My parents were out of town on business and I was left alone in my misery, drinking my dad's beer. As I already told you during the interview, I was on my second bottle when Jim came by."

He took a deep breath and continued, "And as you also know, I talked him into having a beer of his own in celebration of his good news. You're right, he only drank it out of loyalty because he knew that I was bummed about being rejected. It was while he was sipping the beer, obviously not liking the taste, that he told me about his stage fright. I remember him looking at me in panic, saying, 'Nobody knows, but I'm terrified about tonight. I don't think I'll be able to perform with the auditorium full of people staring at me.'"

Sean swallowed a couple of times, then tearing up again as he continued, "A sudden rage came over me. Here was my friend, who, in all four years since I'd known him had always everything going his way. He got straight A's, excelled in any task ever given to him, got accepted to the university of my own choice with a full scholarship, and most agonizing of all, had the girl of my dreams. And now, for the first time in his life, he had something to worry about."

He gulped for air as he kept on, his speech coming in rapid succession as he seemed to re-live the incident. "I needed to vent my anger and quickly thought of something that would make him look like a fool. I told him a little secret of my own, stating that, contrary of what he or everyone else thought, I always had stage fright before sitting on a panel of debate teams. That was all nonsense. I had never experienced any kind of stage fright, but he gobbled it all up as fact. I said that I had a remedy for calming my nerves and making me feel at ease. 'Wait,' I said, 'I'll go get it.'

"I went to my dad's medicine cabinet and took six Vicodin pills and dropped them into a small plastic baggie. Then I gave them to him without telling what kind of pills they were, only that they would do the trick. I recommended that he needed to take two at dinner time, another two shortly before show time, and the last two during intermission. I said that I guaranteed they would work like a charm. To make a point I asked, 'Have you ever seen me nervous or clam up at a debate?' He smiled and answered, 'You were always cool.' I had him sold on those pills and I could see that he already relaxed, just thinking that they would work."

There was the most tragic expression on Sean's face as he said, "When Jim left, he thanked me for being such a good friend. Honest to God, I never meant for him to die, I only wanted to have some fun watching him being humiliated. I pictured him stumbling across the stage, forgetting his lines and singing out of tune. I had never taken any Vicodin myself and had no idea about the proper dosage. I knew that Dad took it for his back pain, and I once heard him mention that if he took too much, it made him drowsy.

"Watching the musical as a spectator in the audience that evening, I was first disappointed. Jim seemed to have it all together. After intermission, I came to the conclusion that he either didn't take the pills, or else they had no effect on him. To my amazement, I actually enjoyed the musical. The last of his solos especially was a treat and for a moment I'd forgotten about the pills."

He sighed and said, "Well, you know the rest. I haven't had a peaceful day since. When I found out what my stupid prank did to Jim, I became tormented by guilt. And the guilty conscience has never left me. I'm actually relieved it's all coming to an end."

I got to my feet and announced, "I'm making a citizen's arrest."

There was no need for me to draw my gun. Sean sat still in his office chair until the authorities showed up and took over, and then he went with them like a lamb to slaughter.

I had already alerted Sergeant Diego of my endeavor before driving to Irvine that morning, so it was easy for her and the local law enforcers to synchronize their undertaking.

The rain had stopped when I walked to where my Jeep was parked. I got in and first called Tho. After hearing my news, he thanked me profusely, expressing that he and his family would forever be in my debt.

Since I was near her university, I decided to inform Melissa in person.

CHAPTER 44

We met again at the Anthill Pub & Grille on the UC Irvine campus. Over the phone I had only mentioned that the cold case was solved and the culprit arrested. Now, over a cup of coffee in between her classes, I told Melissa the sad circumstance of Jim's fate.

She sat up straight, paying keen attention to every word. When my narrative came to an end, she stayed silent for an entire minute with her eyes staring at the wall opposite our table.

Then she burst out, "I knew Jim didn't have an opioid habit and that suicide was out of the question. I also felt sure that nobody had a reason to kill him but it seemed the only logical solution. Now that you're telling me that it was a stupid prank gone wrong, set off by Sean, it almost makes sense."

She slammed her fist down on the table and cried out, "But why? They were best friends, why would Sean want Jim to make a fool of himself onstage?"

My mom's words came to mind and I said, "I'm sure you know from experience that teenagers' emotions can run wild, making them act irrational and irresponsible. It seems that it's all due to hormones."

"Maybe, but Jim was the kindest guy on earth. Sean had no reason to get mad at him."

I stated, "He was plagued by envy."

"Oh, because Jim was accepted at UCI and Sean was not?"

"That too, among other things that came easy to his friend. But the most persistent reason was *you*. He was jealous of Jim's relationship with you."

She did not deny it, just lowered her head.

Then she said, "Sean suffered as much as I did when Jim died, and we comforted one another. Now I realize his misery was from guilt. I knew that he liked me but wanted to keep to a platonic friendship, which he seemed to be fine with."

I knew better, being positive that Sean was still in love with her, remembering his words during our first talk when he mentioned that Melissa's current boyfriend was a jerk, and that he could wait. I was not going to mention this to her, though.

She said, "It hurts that Jim kept his stage fright a secret from me. I would have thought that we were close enough that I'd earned his confidence."

"Maybe he wanted to spare you the worry," I suggested.

She took a long sip of her coffee and then commented, "The trusting and easy-to-manipulate boy that Jim was, I can picture him believing that the pills Sean gave him would cure his butterflies. But what I don't understand is why they actually seemed to have worked. I mean, Vicodin is a painkiller and may slow you down, but I doubt that it has any influence on your psyche. I am 100 percent positive that Jim had no stage fright whatsoever, neither before nor during his performance on opening night. Believe me, I would have known."

I stated, "Of course the Vicodin in and of itself did not cure his stage fright, but I look at it this way: Jim had faith in what his friend assured him, and by the power of suggestion was convinced the pills would make him relax and unafraid to face the audience. And since he believed it, his trust in them worked in his favor. And from what I've gathered, he was able to perform well, until time ran out and his body reacted to the overdose."

Melissa posed her final question, "Did you suspect Sean all along?"

"No. In the beginning, and until proven otherwise, I suspected everyone. Only recently, when I recalled a remark Jim's sister had made early on in my investigation, her words steered me in the right direction. She said, 'You can't force someone to swallow pills.' That's true, I thought, but you can suggest it. And having learned from several people how trusting and gullible Jim was, I strongly suspected that someone made that suggestion to him. For a brief moment I supposed it was you."

"Me?" she asked, wide-eyed.

"During our interview, you denied that Jim had stage fright, which made me suspicious. But you were one of the few people involved I could not come up with having a motive."

"Well, thank you for that!"

"The crucial turn of events was when I realized that the killer need not have been near Jim in the two to three hours before his collapse, if my theory of suggestion was correct. And then I remembered Sean mentioning that his dad had been in the habit of taking strong medicine for his back pain. From that point onward, I started to connect all the dots."

She shook her head and said, "What a waste of a young life! And all because of a stupid hoax from a jealous kid."

She checked her watch and said, "Oops, I'm late for my next class. Thanks for explaining things," and she jumped up and was gone.

CHAPTER 45

Sean Brooks' trial was at the beginning of April and, after the jury selection, only lasted two days. It was a sad event indeed. Sean sat at the defense table, his eyes cast down in remorse and shame. His lawyer, seated next to him, draped an arm around his shoulder in a protective gesture at least twice during the process. The young man's parents sat in the first row behind him. The dad stared stone-faced at the attorney's back, and the mom was red-eyed from crying. The Hoàng family members occupied four seats in the second row behind the prosecution table, all wearing solemn expressions.

The prosecution had lined up the following witnesses to testify: Melissa Van der Molen, Alex Topalian, Zoe Roberts, Sergeant Anna Diego, and myself. I was not in the courtroom during the statements of the others but assumed that the former high school students were questioned about the night of the musical's premiere. I guessed that Sergeant Diego's testimony concerned the initial police report and coroner's findings of three-and-a-half years earlier, as well as the more recent arrest of the defendant.

As a law enforcement officer, I had been called to testify in trials in the past and never enjoyed the chore. Now, with the case being of a personal nature, I had looked forward to the witness stand even less. After being sworn in and lowering myself into the hot seat, I noticed a few familiar faces in the audience besides the Brookses and the Hoàngs.

Diana was there, giving me an encouraging smile. Nelson Montagu, aka Mr. Drama, was seated next to Mike Higginson, and I spotted my ex-partner Rick in the last row. I briefly glanced over to the jury box. Some of the jurors paid attention but others clearly did not. One lady was nonchalantly filing her nails.

The district attorney informed the court that I was a former lieutenant of the sheriff's department, assigned to criminal investigations, and that I had been asked by Tho Hoàng to investigate the closed case.

He proceeded with, "Please state to the jury how you arrived at your findings which led to the defendant's arrest."

So I told the story from A to Z, mostly looking straight ahead. Halfway through the speech, my eyes strayed over to the jurors. Some took notes, others sat up straight and watched me intently. One thing was clear, I had captured their interest. Without exception, the twelve, plus two alternates, paid attention.

At the end of my testimony I faced Sean's attorney in cross-examination. He leaned close to me and said, "Isn't it a fact that you tricked the defendant into admitting you to his apartment, making him believe that you had solved the case but needed to ask him a few questions before revealing the culprit?"

I stated, "No, sir. There was no trickery. I did ask him questions and did in fact reveal *him* as the culprit."

He continued, "And isn't it true that you coaxed him into a confession which, by the way, was not recorded, nor in writing?"

I said, "He gave the confession of his own free will. Granted, it was oral and not officially recorded." I added, "I do have the video on my smartphone if you're interested."

The defense lawyer looked over to the judge and said, "No more questions for this witness, your Honor."

On the next and final day of the trial, the defense attorney called his witnesses. They were both character witnesses. One was a friend of the Brooks' family who had known Sean all his life, the other a former teacher of Sean's at Citadel High School.

The jury deliberated for only two hours to reach a verdict. The foreman stood and officially read, "*We, the jury, find the defendant guilty of involuntary manslaughter.*"

The sentencing followed with the judge defining involuntary manslaughter as a homicide without the intent to kill. The judge also ruled as mitigating factors that the defendant did not pose a great risk to society and that the defendant's age at the time of the crime had been one month short of 18.

He explained further that the gravity of that kind of manslaughter would call for a four-year prison term. The mitigating factor would have reduced it to two years, had the defendant taken immediate responsibility for his act.

Since he did not, and the truth only surfaced after an investigation, the judge pronounced the following sentence: *Three years in a California state prison, plus a $10,000 fine.*

CHAPTER 46

Diana and I had dated several times more since ringing in the New Year on the Queen Mary. We had treated ourselves to things like dining out, seeing a movie, horse races, and having a picnic in the park. I even agreed to a classical music concert, which I ended up enjoying, to my great surprise. Diana had spent one night at my condominium, but even though I had on occasion picked her up at her house, I had never stepped past the entryway.

On Saturday, April 27, she invited me to dinner at her home, located in a classy neighborhood in Pasadena. At the door, she thanked me for the spring flower bouquet with a peck on the cheek.

She did not give me a tour of the two-story Mediterranean house. Instead, she ushered me through the entry hall to an airy open room, saying, "Make yourself comfortable in the den. Dinner will be ready in a few minutes, I'm just tossing a salad," and she vanished through the adjacent dining room towards the kitchen.

I sat down on a comfortable couch and glanced around the room. Straight in front of me, there was a large TV, flanked by shelves containing videos and movies to one side, and a bookcase stacked with hardcover editions on the other. On the walls hung framed prints of contemporary art. I noticed a stand with a large framed photo on a corner pedestal and went to examine it close up. The picture was of a boy with auburn hair, about 12 or 13 years of age. This must be Diana's son, I thought.

I was about to go over to the bookcase and browse through the book titles and authors when she came to fetch me. As I followed her to the dining room she said, "This house is way too big for me, but it's the only thing I was given after the divorce. I'll sell it but haven't gotten around to putting it on the market yet. The commute to Lake View Terrace is 30 to 40 minutes, depending on traffic, so I'll look for something smaller and closer to work."

Before I could comment she motioned me into a chair at the set table and hurried to the kitchen, emerging seconds later, carrying a huge serving dish filled with steaming lasagna in hands clad with oven mitts.

"Wow! Are you planning to feed an army?" I remarked.

"We'll eat what we can and I'll freeze the rest."

During the delicious meal we engaged in light dinner conversation and it was only later, as we lingered over coffee, that we touched on the subject of Sean Brooks.

Diana said, "It goes to show you what an instant of a teen's reckless decision can lead to. High school kids need to be made aware of the grave consequences a prank can have. I'm thinking of giving a presentation about it at Citadel."

I said, "Sean had no idea that his stupid prank would end in his friend dying. I felt bad for him at the trial and still do now, but the verdict of involuntary manslaughter was just, and so was the sentencing."

I looked out the dining room window to the backyard swimming pool and wondered whether she often made use of it.

She also glanced out in that direction and, as if she knew what I was thinking, said, "The pool is a total waste now. I rarely swim in it and certainly don't hold pool parties any longer."

And at last I brought up the subject that was utmost on my mind, saying, "Soon, Connor's time at the camp will be up. On May 16, to be exact. I've agreed to have him stay with me for the summer. He attended classes at camp and should be up to date. Whether or not I'll enroll him at the local high school in Burbank for his senior year depends on how things work out between him and me in the next few months."

She gave me a long, knowing look and said, "You're apprehensive, which is only natural."

I nodded. "I haven't done any parenting in the last ten years. Frankly, I've forgotten how. He was seven when we last lived under the same roof, and now he's almost my height. I doubt that I'm equipped to handle a teen, and possibly a hostile one at that."

"Give yourself some credit. You've handled teenagers in retrospect not too long ago."

"You mean the investigation? Yes, I guess that counts." And after a moment's hesitation I added, "I'm having a hard time dealing with the fact that my son is a juvenile delinquent and that I'll need to treat him with tough love, as they say."

Diana commented, "I'm confident that the six months of camp resulted in a turnaround of his attitude and behavior. Wait and see, he may need less tough love than you think."

After a long pause she said, "If you and I are going to have a future together, what happens with your son concerns me too. In other words, we're in this as a team."

My heart skipped a beat. "Say that again!"

"Which part?"

"The one about us having a future together."

She laughed and stated, "I'm done playing games at my age. We've dated long enough to consider the next step."

"I'm just thinking that with me basically being a blue collar guy, and you - - well, you know what you are - - I don't measure up. And then there are my restrictions, like not being able to play some more physical sports or dance up a storm, and other limitations. You wouldn't want to deal with all that in the long run."

"Don't be an idiot! I don't care about those issues. We are comfortable with one another, which is more important than any of the arguments you just made. And there is not a thing wrong with your lovemaking, if that's what you meant with 'other limitations.'"

"Thanks," I said with a grin.

"Getting back to your son, I'll support you no matter what you decide about his senior year of high school. Meanwhile, give him the benefit of a doubt. He may be easier to handle than you expect. The two of you might enjoy each other's company and have some fun this summer. It may initially be hard, not only for you but also for him, to get accustomed to your roles as father and son. After all, you are basically strangers.

"And remember, friends are of the utmost importance to kids. Teens in particular are social animals, so you need to give him the opportunity to make new pals here in California. Find out what his interests are - - other than partying - - and connect him with the appropriate group of peers."

I remarked, "That's what I like about you, always pointing out the bright side!"

"Speaking of which, you may even enroll him at Citadel High School for the year, getting him ready for college."

I did not mention it but thought that my ex and her current husband might well be able to afford the tuition.

As I left Diana's house hours later, I felt confident in more ways than one.

EPILOGUE

I had to settle something with the Hoàng family. Their convenience store was closed on Mondays, and Jennifer only had morning classes on that day of the week. I arranged to see them at their house on Monday afternoon, April 29.

Upon entering, I first apologized to Tho for taking up his and Lan's time on the only day of the week that they had a bit of free time. He assured me that they did not mind and guided me into the living room where his family was assembled. It was evident that they had been waiting for me, ceremonial teapot and cups at the ready.

Tho performed the duty of host and tea server. As he slowly poured the brew from the teapot into our cups, he said, "This manner of pouring is known in my country as 'high mountain-long river.' It helps the scent of the tea to spread evenly."

While we sipped the lotus tea, Tho remarked, "Enjoying a cup of tea and thinking about life helps people to be good and avoid evil. In the old country, four words are used to describe the phases of tea drinking: *Hòa, Kinh, Thanh,* and *Tịch* which translates to peace, respect for the elderly and friends, tranquility, and leisure."

I was eager to bring up the subject I had come to discuss but also suspected that in the Vietnamese culture it would be considered rude if I jumped right into my agenda. Therefore, I silently drank the tasty brew, studying each person in the room. They all seemed at peace. The painful frown on my friend Tho's face was gone. Part of Lan's sorrow seemed to have left her eyes, and she managed a smile. Grandma appeared to glow. I did not see much change in Jennifer. I still sensed her strong vitality that I'd noticed when we met at the start of my investigation. Again, she willed herself to sit still, and as our eyes met, I imagined her thinking, "Get on with it, already!"

With great formality Tho spoke into the silence and said, "Nick, my family thanks you for what you did for us. We knew all along that Jim's death was not the result of an overdose of drugs, nor a suicide, and believed someone killed him. Thanks to you, we now know the truth. Although shocking, what happened is less painful for us to accept than if we would have learned that somebody willfully had murdered him."

His expression turned even more solemn as he stated, "You have given us closure. We will be forever in your debt."

I decided that now was the time to make my request. I said, "I'm in the process of writing a book of true crime short stories. In fact, I started on the project a long time ago and recently picked it up again. The reason I wanted to meet with all of you today is to ask your permission to include Jim's case in my work. Naturally, I'll also ask for other people's consent, including Sean Brooks', but I'm coming to you first."

Absolute stillness overcame the room. Lan, who had been in the process of bringing the teacup to her lips, stopped in mid-air. Tho stared at me, Jennifer had an amused smirk on her face, and Mai looked bewildered. The latter broke the silence, starting a rapid and loud dialogue between her and her son, who must have explained my words to her. I had forgotten that she was hard of hearing and vouched to speak up from that point onward.

Tho turned to me and said, "I don't like the idea of making a spectacle of my son's fate."

"It goes without saying that I would change all names and places in the book."

"I still don't like it."

"If it gets published and sells well, I would give you a cut from the profit," I coaxed.

"I don't want to make money from Jim's misfortune."

Realizing that my last comment had been the wrong approach, I said, "I'm sure that Jim himself would want other young people to learn from Sean's mistake. If high school kids would read that particular story in my book, they would take to heart what horrible consequences pranks may lead to."

"You have a point there," Tho admitted, and I could tell that he was starting to waver.

I addressed Lan, saying, "What do you think?"

She looked at her husband, then back to me, and stated, "I think you're right. Jim would want you to tell his story. Besides, you helped in giving us closure, the least we can do for you is give our permission."

I hollered, "Mrs. Hoàng, what is your opinion?"

The old lady replied, "You tell story. You say Jim good boy. You say he love grandma!"

"Yes, ma'am. If I get to write it, I will for sure mention that he was a good kid and that he loved his grandma."

Jennifer held thumbs-up with both hands and proclaimed, "You've got my vote!"

Tho finally gave in. "Looks like I'm outnumbered. Go ahead and do it."

I was on the way to my car when Jennifer ran after me and said, "Thank you for not letting on in front of my parents that I believed Jim committed suicide."

"I'll keep that between you and me and won't mention it in the book either."

"Thanks!"

I was already inside the Jeep when she knocked against the driver side window. I rolled it down and she made a request:

"If you ever sell the movie rights to Jim's story in your book, make sure they don't give my part to some clueless airhead."

Stand-Alone Mysteries by Alice Zogg

No Curtain Call
The Ill-Fated Scientist
Accidental Eyewitness
A Bet Turned Deadly

R. A. Huber Mysteries by Alice Zogg

Evil at Shore Haven
Guilty or Not
Murder at the Cubbyhole
Revamp Camp
Final Stop Albuquerque
The Fall of Optimum House
The Lonesome Autocrat
Tracking Backward
Turn the Joker Around
Reaching Checkmate